The Whispering Winds

A novella by

Gloria C. Bishop

DEDICATION

To Lindsay, Tom and Jason. Growing up we tortured
each other, in both good and bad ways. You taught me
about humor and strength and intelligence in the face of
adversity. Without you I wouldn't be the person I am
today.

ACKNOWLEDGMENTS

My ever loving gratitude goes out to the following;

The Imagined Writers group, who kept my spirits high when I didn't think I had it in me.

My Mom. Always in my heart and on my mind.

My team of fabulous beta readers and editors for reading the roughest draft known to man.

My family for putting up with me at my craziest.

Bill for refusing to let me quit and for loving me even when I have on my ugly cry face.

And to my bestie Tracy, I know who has my back.

~~~

Michelle came to consciousness slowly, shocked that she still lived. She didn't move, a stillness learnt from past necessity kept her from betraying the fact that she had awoken. She had no idea where she was, or who might be around. Taking a quick inventory of her pain wracked body she didn't think anything had been broken. Aches existed everywhere on her body, evidence of the bruising that surely covered her. A deep pain in her jaw and inside her mouth told of damage there and an inevitably swollen and puffy face. Injured, but ALIVE she analyzed. She would survive this as she had so many other things.

A shuffling sound to her left let her know that the room was otherwise occupied. Without moving she touched the bed beneath her, soft, smooth fabric met her fingertips, unlike the thin foam that she had slept on for the past eight years. A slight inhale had the scent of oranges suffusing her nose. Definitely not in the trailer anymore. Ever cautious she cracked one eye a sliver; enough to see soft light filtering through an eyelet style curtain that moved in the breeze, giving brief glimpses into a forest that spanned beyond the window.

She had no idea where she might be and fought for control of her breathing and her body, she would NOT panic. A soft voice invaded her ears before she could freak out.

1

"I know you're awake." The quiet, calm female voice spoke. "You are safe here."

Michelle opened her eyes warily, meeting the gaze of the woman. Her brown eyes were almost hidden behind the fringe of black bangs as she looked back steadily. "My name is Calia. I've brought you some orange juice." She tilted her head towards a glass that sat on an ornate silver tray along with a bagel, knife and small bowl that Michelle assumed contained butter or jam. The tray stood on the bedside table within easy reach of Michelle. "Don't move too fast you are still injured, and you have been asleep for some time. I wouldn't want you to get dizzy. If you are hungry there is a fresh bagel there as well."

Michelle's eyes flickered to the tray and then with mistrust at the woman standing a cautious distance away. "Where am I?" Her voice scratched at her throat painfully.

"This is The Whispering Winds. It is an artist's retreat just outside of Morrisburg Ontario." Calia's black hair flowed over her shoulder, she moved slowly treating Michelle as tenderly as a frightened animal.

"How did I get here?" Michelle demanded, hating the weakness in her voice.

"I found you barely clinging to a log in the river that flows along the edge of my property. I am a ... healer and I brought you to my home to help you. Can you tell me your name?" Again her soft and soothing voice only served to irritate Michelle.

"Michelle." She struggled to sit up, cursing the pain that filled her even more now that she moved. "And while I thank you for your hospitality, I need to go." Spots danced in front of her eyes as the world seemed to tilt on its axis. A physical and mental weariness threatened to take over but through sheer willpower Michelle pushed it back and attempted to stand.

"Michelle." Worry filled Calia's voice as she moved closer. "You are in no shape to go anywhere. I don't know what happened to you but I assure you that here, you are safe." She reached out to touch Michelle's arm when she teetered slightly but Michelle flinched away. "You are safe. Please," her agonized voice drifted over the room. "Get back into bed. Let us take care of you. You aren't in any shape to go anywhere."

Realizing the futility of attempting to leave when she couldn't even stand on her own Michelle lowered herself back onto the bed, defeat in her posture. Even her mind felt fuzzy and in this state she couldn't escape anywhere. She needed time to heal, to regain her energy. Taking a deep breath and wincing at the twinge in her ribs she knew she'd have to trust this woman, for now. If she ran she wouldn't make it far and if Phelon, she cringed at the mere thought of him, if he found her she would never escape again.

Without speaking Calia seemed to sense her acquiescence and handed her the glass of orange juice before moving away to a safe distance. She hummed lightly

3

as she watched, a tune that calmed Michelle as she took a tentative sip of the juice, disturbed that the tiny cup required the use of both her hands to hold it without dropping it. Bright orange exploded on Michelle's tongue, the juice was freshly squeezed and tasted like heaven after the scanty meals she had had recently. Knowing she needed sustenance to heal she drank the rest down.

"Michelle, please sleep. It will help. I have others here who will help you, and when you wake, we will all endeavor to make you healthy again."

Overwhelmed with weariness Michelle set down her now empty glass and palmed the knife off the tray as she lay back down clutching her weapon to her chest. Making sure she faced the door she watched out of the corner of her eye as Calia pulled the curtains closed, darkening the room and with a sigh of defeat Michelle closed her eyes and let sleep claim her.

~~~

Unable to open her eyes Michelle drifted in and out of unconsciousness for what felt like forever. She surfaced enough to hear voices in the room next to her, and recognized Calia's soft tones. "I've done what I can for now. When she awakens I will heal her again."

A man's voice followed. "Why did you bring her here? Calia, you told me we'd have use of the house. Now you bring a human stranger in."

"She's just so broken." A sigh. "And not only physically. Although that is bad enough. Surely you can sense that mentally she's taken a beating. Even in sleep she is still clutching that knife like it's her only lifeline. You and Dawn can help her in ways I have no ability to."

"I can't. Damn it Calia. I can't." The man's voice held so much pain that in her semi-conscious state Michelle ached for him.

"You can. I know it. I have faith in you." Calia continued talking but the voices faded away as Michelle went under again.

~~~

"*How* did she end up here?" This new harsh female voice cut through the fog of unconsciousness in Michelle's brain.

"I found her floating in the river, she was unconscious and barely clinging to a log." Calia spoke quietly but clearly enough for Michelle to hear.

"So we know nothing about her?" A gruff male voice spoke. "How do you know she means no harm to us? To you? Why didn't you just call the human police?"

"We know she has been beaten to within an inch of her life. Ray, we know she needs help." The second female voice spoke. "We also know she's human but with some sort of extra. Human plus shall we say. There are magic's surrounding her that are thick and definitely not in a nice way, she needs us. You also know that the land will tell Calia if this woman is a threat. And we aren't about to turn her away. You know as well as I that Calia couldn't turn her away."

"Awe, Jesus, Dell I didn't suggest that. Just odd, the whole situation." Ray sounded abashed.

Michelle fought the fog that came for her trying desperately to open her eyes but losing the battle she drifted away once more.

~~~

𝒟awn paced the length of the living room, her booted feet leaving a light pattern in the plush carpet. "What do you want to do?" She asked, glancing at Mason.

Mason scowled. "I want to leave. To run away. Dammit I came here to get away from humans, not be housed so closely with one."

"I know." Dawn sighed.

"But how can I?" Mason shifted his large body on the tiny but comfortable loveseat he sat on. "Calia has never asked for help before. She jumped at the chance to have us here. To give me a safe place to recover." His voice was bitter as he spat out recover.

"She knows what we can do?" Dawn asked quietly skirting the issue of Mason's recovery. They had been here for nearly a month and he had lost the haunted look that had plagued him when they first arrived.

Mason nodded. "In general terms yes. Specifically I don't think so. Unless she's met another Cubus that is."

A sound from the doorway had both looking up to see Calia flanked by a large man they had never met before. "Sorry." Calia smiled apologetically. "I didn't mean to interrupt. And no I don't know specifically what you can do. That's why we came over. This is my friend Ray." She motioned to the silent man standing beside her. "Can we come in?"

Dawn looked over the man, she estimated him to be the same height as herself, around 5'8", relatively short for a man. That might make people look past him, but Ray stood proud and tall, his fine physique and arresting green eyes made him appear taller. *Damn*, Dawn thought with a sigh of appreciation as she looked him over closely, *his muscles have muscles.* Then with an inaudible sniff she smelled the air and knew that he was one of the Hidden. The same as Mason and herself and even Cali. This man wasn't even a human, he was something other. Dawn didn't recognize the scent but she knew as sure as she knew her hair was short that Ray was special which explained his presence.

Pulling her head from the clouds she looked at Mason who gave an imperceptible nod and with a warmer smile she motioned the two into the room. "It's your house Calia come on in."

Calia laughed lightly, "While you are staying here it is your place. I wouldn't feel right barging in. Well," She grinned. "I would do it if needed but I wouldn't feel right about it."

They pulled chairs from the kitchen table and set them in the living room across from where Mason sat. In a gesture of support Dawn forced herself to stop pacing and moved to sit beside Mason, lending him her strength.

"So as you can tell," Calia started, "Ray is a Hidden as well. He is a nymph. He is also one of my best friends. When I need advice he is who I call."

Both Mason and Dawn nodded a greeting at Ray who, unsmiling, returned the gesture.

8

"So let's get right down to it. I found this Michelle and she needs somewhere to stay. She needs help. She needs me, and by extension you."

"I understand that." Dawn leaned towards Calia, her elbows resting comfortably on her knees. "I am a counsellor I can see that she needs us and I don't want to say no. But my main concern right now has to be Mason."

Mason grunted in what Dawn wasn't sure was agreement or disgust at the fact that he needed her help.

"I get that. Trust me I do. But Mason looks so much better than he did." Calia looked at Mason. "You look wonderful in fact. The Whispering Winds has been good for you. I didn't invite you here to use your skills or to stick you with a sick human. I just don't know anyone else to call on. She is so very broken. It hurts me to see it."

Ray cleared his throat. "Okay people." His voice was clipped and seemed slightly British in his tight pronunciations. "Perhaps you can bring me up to speed. Who is this girl? And why do you think that Dawn and Mason here can help her? And finally why should you help her or risk yourselves to do so?"

Calia closed her eyes briefly before turning to face Ray. "I began the healing of her physical wounds, which there are plenty. She had been beaten to within an inch of her life. As I healed her I know there is mental damage that I cannot help. She is broken, inside and out. She awoke briefly. Her name is Michelle and she is a skittish thing. We

9

don't know much. Although she is human, there is something 'other' about her. She is terribly weak, and I have kept her in a healing trance for much of the week since I brought her here. Whoever did this to her has left hooks in her psyche that he will be able to track. I believe they will come for her, and probably soon, and she needs to be ready."

Ray nodded as he digested what Calia said. "Okay." He finally spoke. "I understand why she is here. I don't understand why you haven't called the human police or taken her to a hospital. Surely they would be more equipped to deal with her."

"I cannot allow a person that the universe brought me to leave in such a state." Calia's voice rose slightly. "I am a healer. It is what the land demands of me and what I want, need to do. The fates brought her to me to help and dammit I will help her. I cannot turn her away."

With a soft smile, Ray held up his hands in defeat. "All right. Calm yourself. I am just trying to understand. So now I see why you are involved. Now why are you bringing these nice folks into your drama?" He nodded his head towards Dawn and Mason.

"First because they are staying in my home. It is the only place with an open bedroom. All the cabins are rented out. My home is the only suitable place to put Michelle. So that puts them in close proximity. And second because they are Cubus," Calia's voice dropped off and she looked beseechingly at Dawn.

Dawn took up the imaginary talking stick. "I think I would be better equipped to address this part of the answer. Have you ever met a Cubus?' She looked at Ray and when he shook his head she continued. "That's not hard to believe. The Cubus have always been rare." At Ray's confused look she clarified. "I am a Succubus and Mason is an Incubus. And together we are a whole Cubus."

"Do you mind telling me more about your species? Specifically how the Whole versus Half works?" Calia asked.

"Sure." Dawn grinned and sat back. "Each Cubus, be it Succubus or Incubus is born with half a soul. Very rarely they find their other half and are finally Whole. It's like finding a part of yourself that you didn't know you missed."

"So are you a couple then?" Ray's eyebrows were furrowed.

"No." Dawn laughed. "We aren't. We are two halves of a whole, but it's not sexual. It's more of a friendship, we share emotions and feedings and such. We are each other, together we make one complete being."

"As to feeding, is there anything that should concern us? I mean," Ray turned bright red. "According to what I've seen and read you guys feed exclusively during sex and it can prove fatal to your meals." He looked at the floor discomfort radiating from him.

11

"No, we fed before coming here. Also it's really not what you've seen on television. We feed on energy, on emotions. Admittedly sexual energy tastes the best, but we make due with what is available. Neither Mason nor I have ever killed a human with a feeding. Your guests are safe with us." Mason shifted uncomfortably but Dawn ignored him as she spoke.

"Okay then, although I knew Calia wouldn't have brought you here if you weren't trustworthy, I had to ask." Ray turned to Mason. "And do you ever talk?"

His husky voice answered. "I do. But typically Dawn is better at verbalizing things so I let her take the lead. Maybe instead of talking about the Cubus etymology we should talk about why you need us. What you think we can do for her, and frankly why I should give a shit."

"I know you don't feel the same as I do for this poor woman." Calia looked straight into Mason's eyes. "And I know you are here running from something that happened to you. But you are still the same Mason I knew in school. That Mason would never leave a person hurting. You haven't changed that much. If you can't do it for her, or for yourself do it for me. I am asking you. As my old friend, please help me."

"So what do you need us to do?" Mason spoke softly.

*M*ichelle opened her eyes slowly, pleased with the strength coursing through her. She thought she could finally get up. She had no idea how long she had been unconscious but it had been too long. Vague memories, that felt like dreams filtered in her brain bits of conversations spoken around her and she processed all that had been said. Whoever her rescuers were they probably meant her no harm but they wouldn't be safe as long as Phelon came for her. Slowly she stood, glad that while still weak she could stand on her own. Frowning, she fingered the soft night gown she wore a longing overcoming her until she shook herself. It couldn't be helped, she needed to get away and this pretty gown would only be a hindrance. She opened the closet and was happy to discover a woman's t-shirt and yoga pants in a size that may not have been hers but fit well enough. She slipped them on ignoring the still vivid bruises that dotted her body. Michelle took a breath distressed to discover how out of breath and worn out she felt simply from getting dressed. Steeling herself she squared her shoulders determined to ignore the weakness that infused every fiber of her being.

She hid her knife behind her, because while she was relatively sure that danger didn't exist right now, she couldn't take any chances. She moved cautiously towards the door. Cracking it open she looked into the main room of what appeared to be a cabin. The décor had the look of rustic charm, but seemed at the same time too expensive looking to be authentic.

Across the room Calia sat cross legged in an overstuffed armchair, she spoke in a quiet voice to a man and woman who sat on the couch with their backs to Michelle. She glanced back into the bedroom debating the feasibility of crawling out the window. Deciding against the idea, knowing she couldn't handle the pain of trying to climb that far, she quickly studied the living room, noting the location of the exit then taking a slow breath to avoid the pain in her ribs she stepped out into the room.

Calia immediately stood up. "Michelle. I am so glad you're awake. Please come sit." She moved from the comfortable seat, giving it up for Michelle to sit. She motioned to the chair and stepped back so as to avoid touching Michelle as she made her way across the room.

"I'd like to introduce you to Dawn and Mason. They have a special ability that will help heal you." Calia pulled a chair up and sat casually.

Michelle looked at the couple sitting on the couch. Her eyes going quickly to the woman, Dawn. She sat erect on the couch, a half smile curving sensual full lips. Her almost non-existent hair buzzed in a military cut served to make her large blue eyes stand out more. She wore jeans and a t-shirt and large sparkling earrings which shimmered in the soft light and her alabaster skin glowed. A tingle went through her as she looked at the stunning, long and lean woman. Confused by the emotions that flooded her she glanced at the man.

Her breath caught in her throat as she took in his wide shoulders and mussed up hair that wasn't blond, brown or red but rather a combination of all the above. He lounged on the couch, a frown on his handsome face and if Michelle read him right he seemed to be trying to be less intimidating. He had a tan that showed pure good health and a jawline that could cut through butter. His bright green eyes stared back at Michelle and she looked away confused by the thread of lust that rushed through her when she looked at both of these stunning creatures.

Calia handed Michelle another glass of orange juice. "Drink this, it will help with your strength." Michelle took the cup, grateful to have something to do besides be the dowdy creature compared to the three specimens of beauty and health that sat with her.

Her voice soft, Dawn spoke. "Michelle, it's very nice to meet you. I wish it had been under better circumstances but we will be able to help you. I guarantee it."

"Remember, you are safe here." Calia assured her. "But if we are going to be able to help and protect you, we need to know more about you. What happened to you?"

Michelle stiffened up and shook her head. She didn't want to talk about it, she didn't want to think about it, she wanted to run away and forget. Panic rose hard and fast in her chest, her breathing becoming tight. Just as the fear became too much it drained away, siphoning off her body and mind as though a plug had been pulled in a tub.

"Solotke," Mason spoke quietly his voice hesitant but determined. "No harm will come to you. I vow to you, we will keep you safe. If you talk about what happened we can help." While Michelle knew she should be afraid of the big man she found herself instead calmed and comforted by his words.

"No one can help me." She whispered. "I need to leave before I put all of you in danger."

"You aren't going anywhere." Mason growled to which Michelle jumped slightly and he cursed under his breath. "You need healing. We can help."

Dawn leaned forward her hands out. "Michelle, I promise no harm will come to you when you are with us." Her blue eyes bored into Michelle's. "Please let us help you."

"How?" Michelle fought against the comfort that threatened to take away her wits, holding onto the mistrust so deeply ingrained in her.

The three looked at each other and finally Dawn spoke. "Something magical happened to you. Something paranormal, right?" Michelle nodded slightly. "Okay, so you know that magic exists. First Calia is a Dryad, you have the good fortune of being found on her property, and she has been healing you physically which is why you are moving around. Without her abilities you would be in much worse shape. Mason and I are Cubus. What that means is that we can take bad emotions, bad energy and convert it into good. We suck the bad memories out, leaving them like a dream, or faded as though they were ancient history. Your energies are dangerously low, we will help to replenish them."

"But it helps, makes it easier on both you and us, if you talk about it." Mason added. "That brings the emotions to the forefront and doesn't make retrieving them as difficult. That doesn't mean you have to talk about everything but trust us when we say you will feel much better if you help the process along. That and with protecting you, it will help. The more we know the better prepared we can be."

Michelle studied the wooden floor intently. Finally she asked, "So you just suck out the bad stuff leaving only good?"

"Sort of." Dawn clarified. "We soften the effects, you will still be you and your memories still yours, but they won't be as sharp edged. They won't hurt as much. Our type of healing will speed your recovery immensely. What would normally require years of therapy will only take days with us, we leave the harmful memories so faded. It will also help with any PTSD, making it almost nonexistent. We aren't mind readers though so you talking about it helps us figure out which memories to soften, where to direct our energy."

17

Again Michelle thought for a long time. Then fighting the tears that threatened to overcome her eyes she asked. "Why? I'm nobody, you don't know me. You don't know anything about me. Why would you do that for me?"

~~~

*M*ason nearly growled out loud in anger at her question. How little love had she known in her life that she would wonder why someone would do a good thing for her? He forced the tension from his limbs and remained outwardly calm.

From the moment he had seen Michelle he had been drawn to her. His initial reticence about helping her dissolved instantaneously. While he was still nervous about his ability to not harm her unintentionally he hid the fact as well as he was able. He had to appear to be as strong as Michelle needed. Without that appearance of calm and power she would bolt. She called to him, making Mason want nothing more than to help and keep her safe. The moment she had appeared in the doorway so fragile looking a pang of pure lust and a soul deep longing had shot through him. He had a hard time keeping his eyes off her and not trying to wrap her up in his arms so that no one could ever hurt her again. His body surged with desire that he forced down with an iron will.

Her tiny fame didn't reach five foot tall, with waist length pitch black hair and almond shaped eyes that showed a misery, a wariness that he wanted to erase. The bruises that dotted her dark skin made him beyond furious. He wanted to put her behind him and protect her with all that he had. Never before had Mason experienced a reaction to a woman like this and he clamped down on his instinct to hold her tight. The tears that brimmed in her eyes were nearly his undoing, he couldn't speak as a protective urge overwhelmed him.

Beside him he could see Dawn reacting the same way. She leaned towards Michelle and answered her question. "Oh honey, you deserve so much. I am a counselor, this is what I do for a living. I help people, and I want nothing more than to help you."

"No one does things for free." Michelle muttered. "What do you get out of it?"

Dawn inhaled slowly. "First and foremost we get to help you. It is my calling, and to a lesser degree, Masons. We want to help. You are right though we do also get something out of it. As Cubus, we feed on energies. It gives us sustenance. We return the energies to you, cleaned and less toxic. We can't heal your physical hurts, that is what Calia is doing, but we can help make you stronger energetically and ready for what is sure to come. We can help to heal your insides. We want to help heal you."

"We want to help you." Mason added in a low gravelly

voice. "Let us help you."

Michelle took a long time thinking, and Mason didn't show his edginess as he waited for her answer. Instead he studied her profile, taking note of the beautiful tilt of her chin. Her darker skin showed clear evidence of her Native ancestry, but underneath the darker tones hung a pallor of unhealthiness. Even after a week of magical, healing sleep she had dark smudges under her eyes and it looked like she spent far too long indoors. Her eyes were the color of warm milk chocolate and the wariness in them lended a knowledge far older than her physical years.

"Okay." Michelle whispered. "So what do we need to do?" Her eyes flickered and filled with embarrassment as she reached a hand down to her side and removed a steak knife that she had tucked in between her hip and the arm of the chair. She carefully set it on the table beside her, still within reach but not currently in hand. Mason nearly cheered at the trust it showed on her part to put her weapon to the side.

"Why don't you start by telling us about your younger years?" She smiled softly. "We'll start nice and easy."

"Okay." Michelle seemed to square her shoulders, her huffed breath told Mason this would be anything but easy. "I am obviously First Nations," she waved a hand towards her face. "But I have never been on a reservation. I grew up in the system. Foster home after foster home. Never knowing my place. Always wanting to find a family but I was never good enough." Her voice dropped to near a whisper and Mason had to lean slightly forward to hear her words. "By the time I turned sixteen I lived in my thirtieth house. I had grown into a pain in the ass teenager, a trouble maker, who wouldn't?" Her eyes briefly met Mason's before she looked away. "I went to my last home three days before my sixteenth birthday. The Chints were, well very Hollywood typical foster parents. In it for the money, not caring at all about the kids. They tended to get a little, okay a lot, punchy when they were drinking. And they were always drinking." Her eyes turned inwards as her memories took over. After a few long minutes she spoke again. "So I ran away. I couldn't take it anymore and I figured myself to be an adult, big and bad enough to be on my own." Her voice died off and Mason could sense the energy in the room shift as Dawn sifted the emotions and moved them towards a more distant memory. Mason sniffed the energy, what Michelle shared already felt distant and he didn't need to soften it. The root of the problem belonged elsewhere. More recent and horrifying.

"That's all ancient history though." Michelle confirmed his thinking with her words. "It kind of lays the back ground for what happened next." She shifted on her seat uncomfortable.

"Why don't you take a drink of that juice?" Mason suggested quietly. "It'll make you feel better. The energies are moving and that's a great start. Take a breath. It will be okay." Her eyes flew to him, misery over laying the fear in them.

"Thank you." She whispered. "Would you mind telling me about yourselves while I catch my breath?" She took a sip and looked expectantly between him and Dawn.

Dawn spoke first. "As I said I am a counsellor, I work at a woman's shelter in Toronto. Mason here is between jobs he used to be a bartender though. So he's a counsellor of sorts as well, just in a different capacity." She smiled winningly as Michelle took another sip of the tangy juice. "What else would you like to know?"

The three of them talked lightly for the next hour getting Michelle to relax around them and then they served up the dinner that Calia had thoughtfully had brought to the cottage. The retreat was full and there was often a dinner served in the pavilion but tonight Calia had pulled rank and stepped away to spend more time with healing Michelle. She told them she had left her friends and staff in charge.

While they talked Mason could sense Calia's healing energies swirling around Michelle. It was a subtle soft green energy that smelled lightly of magic and moss, nothing that would affect the conversation nonetheless Mason noted it. Calia said very little, staying to the background and doing what Mason assumed was a gentle kind of distance healing while Mason and Dawn distracted Michelle with casual conversation. He looked again at Michelle, a burst of doubt in his mind at his ability to keep his promise in regards to her safety. He would die before allowing anyone else to hurt her, but could he stop himself?

~~~

*D*awn could sense her pain and longed more than anything to take it from Michelle and make her whole again. Over the years she had counselled so many victims and she had never reacted this strongly about anyone before.

After dinner they had sent Michelle to bed as her energies were waning. Dawn knew that tomorrow would be a big day of healing, both physical and mental and she knew also she needed to sleep herself to have the strength to help Michelle the way she deserved. Before she climbed into the tiny sleeping loft she looked at Mason as he stared at the door to the bedroom with an intensity she hadn't seen before.

"Are you okay?" She asked quietly.

Mason nodded. "I want to help her. I'm terrified but I can't seem to stop myself. From the moment she first looked at me I knew I couldn't walk away."

"Me neither." Dawn agreed. Internally she cheered to see Mason so connected, so alive again. For the past month she had worried he would never return to his usual personality and today she saw glimpses of it again. "You know you can do this, don't you?"

"I can only hope that I can control myself." Mason's voice was so low Dawn had to strain to hear it.

"You can and you will." She walked over and placed a reassuring hand on his shoulder. "I believe in you."

Mason closed his eyes briefly. "I don't deserve your faith."

"Another area where we'll agree to disagree." They stood in silence for long moments.

Mason looked at her and tilted his head. "Tell me you don't feel it too." Immediately Dawn knew he spoke of the intense attraction to Michelle.

"Oh I never said that. There is something about her." Her loins clenched at the thought of the broken young woman sleeping on the other side of the door. She knew that professionally she should keep a distance, that Michelle had been through so very much and needed space to recover. Dawn could barely restrain herself from wrapping the beautiful woman in her arms and forcing away all her pain.

She knew she should have guilt about the surge of lust that thinking about Michelle drew through her body however she couldn't do it. Her soul cried out to the black haired beauty.

"Is it the same for you?" Mason asked quietly.

"If you mean, do I think that she is our mate? Then

yes. She is..." Dawn's voice died unsure how to describe the completion that the three of them being in the same room brought her.

"Yeah." Mason muttered in agreement. "I need her like I've never needed anything in my entire life. My entire body is screaming for us to mate her. To love her, to protect her and comfort away all the hurts she's had." He paused. "She's been hurt by men. And I cannot bear to be another in a line of males who have let her down and injured her."

Dawn nodded. "You won't let her down. You won't hurt her. You couldn't. Ever." Dawn's voice allowed no argument. "And while she is responding to you, she is still more leery of you because you are male. I hate to be that blunt, but it is what it is. We'll find out more tomorrow. She needs us too."

"I agree. And as much as I want to be there for her right now she needs you more. I have to take the backseat here, which will also give me time to ensure that I won't inadvertently harm her. It kills me to say it, but I know it's true. It will take more than a day to break down her barriers."

"Until then, we need to keep her safe and help her heal." Dawn said with quiet conviction.

~~~

*M*ichelle woke slowly and cautiously, opening her eyes a minute amount at a time, an ingrained habit from her past. Finally deciphering the safety of the room she sat up, immediately she knew she was much better, physically at least. With a quick examination she looked over her body, pleasantly surprised by the amount the bruises had faded overnight.

She stood carefully and made her way to the attached bath, a beautiful room with chocolate brown ceramic tiles on the floors and walls, a double sink perched above the quartz countertop, a hidden commode and large skylight that let in the natural light. An entire baseball team could fit in the huge corner tub. The walk in tiled shower had a rainfall head, a bench seat and a skylight of its own. Shaking her head at the turn of events in her life, this bathroom alone equaled the size of the trailer she had spent the last eight years locked inside.

Deciding she couldn't wait any longer to be clean she stripped off the pajamas she wore and turned on the warm water. Stretching as the spray touched her skin she sighed at the heavenly sensations. She quickly but thoroughly used the provided almond and jasmine scented body wash rubbing gently over the still bruised areas.

She spent a few minutes washing and rinsing her hair. As soon as she felt the telltale weakness tremor through her limbs she turned off the water, grabbing a fluffy towel from the nearby warming rack. She wrapped one towel around her body, and with a sigh at the indulgence she took a second towel and wrapped the length of her hair in it. After taking care of a few necessities she grabbed the hairbrush and stepped back into the bedroom to sit on the comfortable bed to brush out her hair.

Trying to reach up to brush her tangled hair a sharp pain winged across her ribs and she flinched. Grimacing with determination she ignored the pain and lack of strength that threatened and forced the brush through the ends of her long locks.

After a few minutes of trying she let her arms drop to her lap. Even this small thing she couldn't manage. Tears filled her eyes, which she dashed away angrily. Damn it she'd escaped, she had survived and now she cried like some baby who had never lived through anything negative. Now when she could see the light of freedom she broke down because of a little resulting physical fragility.

No matter how firmly she repeated these things to herself she couldn't make the tears stop. They flowed down her cheeks and slipped down her neck, sliding under the edge of the towel as she sat there trying to find the strength to finish brushing her hair.

The door opened and Michelle didn't have the will to

look up and see who had intruded. She didn't want anyone to see her weakness and the evidence of her tears.

"Michelle? What's wrong?" Dawn moved towards the bed, dropping to her knees in front of Michelle. "Tell me."

"I can't." Michelle whispered, motioning with the brush. "I'm such a wuss. I can't even brush my hair."

"No need to cry. Allow me." Dawn gently pried the brush from Michelle's hand then she crawled on the bed behind her. Her legs surrounded Michelle's hips, with a start she realized she could feel the warmth from her womanhood pressing against her backside. She had never been attracted to any woman and confusion filled her at the thoughts that encompassed her mind whenever in Dawn's vicinity. Lust was a foreign emotion for Michelle - why all of a sudden did she clench at the sight of not just Dawn, a woman, but also Mason, not just a man, but a huge man who could easily physically overpower her. She shook her head slightly, unsure of what strangeness affected her brain.

"It's okay. I'm only going to brush your hair." Dawn's voice whispered in her ear as the brush began moving gently through the long tresses. She sighed and relaxed against Dawn, letting her take over. She hummed as she worked a light tune that soother Michelle.

"You have the most beautiful hair." Dawn whispered, sending goose bumps down Michelle's body. She shook her hair slightly in denial. Emotions swamping her again, frustration at the weakness, fear of discovery by Phelon, lust: confusion over said lust, and a longing for love, for family. It had been years since she had hoped, since she had dreamed and the emotions overtook her as Dawn slowly and gently separated the tresses of her hair.

Dawn finished with her hair and slowly, carefully wrapped her arms around Michelle. She hugged her like Michelle had never experienced in her whole life and unable to prevent them, the tears started all over. Tears at what should have been her life, what she should have experienced, the loveless child she had been. Dawn held her gently but firmly, her embrace tight as though she could glue together the bits of Michelle that were splintered from her past.

Michelle fought a sob and turned in Dawn's arms as Dawn murmured soothing words and held her. Her body wracked and shook with long held emotions that she hadn't let loose before and Dawn ran her fingers gently up and down her back.

Finally after the purging of tears slowed Michelle tilted her head back staring into Dawn's wide bright blue eyes. This close she could see the variety of blues that swirled together and formed what looked like storm clouds in her eyes. The contact lasted for a long while until Dawn gently wiped the vestiges of her tears off Michelle's cheeks.

"Sometimes crying is good. It releases the pent up

emotions, frees us from the bondages of being normal, from expectations." She looked at Michelle a fierceness as she interrupted what Michelle had been about to say. "Don't you apologize."

"Okay." Michelle whispered and a small smile took her lips. She became aware that she laid between another woman's legs, their bodies pressed against one another in intimate contact, with only a single thin towel separating her nakedness. She flushed and pulled away but not before noticing what appeared to be an answering lust to match her own in the swiftly darkening blue eyes. Dawn let her go slowly and seemingly with reluctance.

"How's the weakness?" Dawn helped Michelle to the edge of the bed once more.

Michelle shrugged without speaking, she didn't want to admit the depth of her fragility. Her body seemed to drain all motivation, all her energy within moments. The frustration of thinking she was better and then suddenly wilting without the strength to lift her hand filled her with anger and helplessness.

"I can tell it's bad. Let me help you get dressed."

Michelle flushed at the thought and spared a moment to be incredibly grateful for her darker skin that would hide any redness. She couldn't be seen naked by this gorgeous woman who would surely laugh at her shorter legs and rounder figure.

Without noticing Michelle's dismay Dawn stood and bounded to the closet. She returned with a repeat of what Michelle had worn yesterday. She walked back and dropped to her knees in front of Michelle.

"I understand you are shy I promise to do this with as much respect for your modesty as possible. You need help. I am here to help you." She placed her hands gently on Michelle's knees sending a shock of electricity and desire coursing through Michelle. Her shock filled eyes flew to Dawns beseeching ones. "Let me."

Almost imperceptivity Michelle nodded her agreement and Dawn immediately set the yoga pants on the floor slipping them around her feet. She helped Michelle to stand, and then slid the pants up her legs, her fingers only touching the clothing. Once she reached Michelle's upper thighs, just under the edge of the towel, she let Michelle take over yanking the pants up the rest of the way. She fought a deep mortification at the thought of not only going commando, but that Dawn knew she wore no under garments. She fought her dismay, she owned nothing and only wore what had been available in the closet.

Dawn stood with the t-shirt held in her graceful hands. "Okay, arms up." Michelle raised her arms slowly, and Dawn quickly slid the cotton material over her head and arms pulling it down to her waist and then helping to remove the towel from underneath. Only once she had her clothes back on did Dawn touch the bare skin on her arm.

"See modesty kept. Even though it damned near killed me, because you are so very lovely." Her voice a faint whisper that touched Michelle's soul. "I must tell you how very attracted to you I am. I won't let it interfere with helping you, but you need to know." Her fingers lightly brushed Michelle's cheek.

"I'm-" Michelle broke off and looked away. "I've never felt like this about anyone. I'm not gay."

"What we have isn't about gay or straight. It's beyond those small minded matters. It's about souls connecting and knowing one another. It's about the person you are inside your body not whether you have a penis or vagina. I'm drawn to you. What is between us is about the people we are not the skin we are wearing. I could no more resist you and my attraction to you than I could resist breathing. It wouldn't matter if you were male, female, unicorn, werewolf or vampire. I find the essence that is you irresistible. It's you." Her fingers continued to brush across Michelle's skin softly. "I know you aren't ready for that yet. But I didn't want you to think that the attraction I know you're experiencing is one sided. I know you don't understand it yet but you are our mate."

"What does that mean?" Michelle asked timidly.

"Mason and I are each two halves of a whole. Together we have one single soul. Incubus and Succubus together form the Cubus. And together they find their mate. The one person in the world meant for them. You,

Michelle are that person for Mason and me."

"How can you know that?" Michelle fought the fear in her voice to no avail.

"We just do. We felt it from the moment we met you." Dawn paused. "I hesitated on telling you this now but I feel you have the right to know what I feel. This connection between us is more than sexual. More than anything I've ever felt in my life. We won't push you. Even if you never have more than friendly feelings for us, know that you are the one for us."

After the room filled with silence Michelle shifted so she looked at Dawn. "Honestly that terrifies me. I am trying to be strong and fight for my life here and you are talking about soul mates. I don't know if I can ever be the person you both need. I don't know if I can even be the person that I need."

"We'll figure that out. Together." Dawn's firm voice told Michelle of her resolve, her determination. "There is more that you need to know, but for now that is enough to process."

She leaned over and lightly touched her soft full lips to Michelle's in a kiss that seemed both a pledge and a promise. She kept it chaste and quick but nonetheless Michelle's heart quickened and her breathing stuttered in her chest.

Dawn smiled and stood back taking Michelle's hand

33

and led her from the room.

~~~

*D*awn watched Michelle as they ate the breakfast that had been delivered along with a note from Calia letting them know there was a communal dinner this evening in the pavilion and she thought it would do them all good to attend. Mason, Dawn and Michelle were sitting on the small front porch area with coffees in hand and croissants, yogurt and fruit on the tiny table in front of them.

Amazed at the level of restraint she had shown earlier, one brush of Michelle's lips against her own, and the rightness of her pressed against Dawn's body had been enough that her Succubus nature had almost won out. Instead she reigned in the urges, knowing without a doubt that Michelle was not ready for any sexual contact. Mason had raised his eyebrows knowingly when they had come out of the room but managed to keep his mouth shut. The thought of scaring her away terrified Dawn, she was the one woman meant to be their soul mate and Dawn couldn't live with herself if she hurt her.

A comfortable and peaceful silence had reigned through breakfast with each of them caught in their own thoughts. Dawn found it very soothing to look out at the beautiful forest and watch the breeze play with the leaves.

Finally, although she didn't want to break the peaceful quiet that had settled over them, she turned to the others. "Well, we should probably get going for today. Are you ready for your next session?"

Michelle paled with nerves but she nodded bravely. "Same as yesterday?" She asked.

"Essentially yes. We need you to take up on your story. Today Mason is going to concentrate on converting the energy while I focus on making sure you are talking."

Mason took over the narrative. "I am a little different than Dawn in that to return your energy to you cleansed, I will need to touch you." At Michelle's look of panic he hastily added. "It can be your hands. A small physical contact so that I can send everything back to you. Dawn really is better at drawing the story out, drawing the emotions out, then I change them and return them. It's cyclical."

Michelle took a deep breath and nodded with a whispered, "Okay." They all stood and returned to the living room. This time Michelle sat facing Dawn on the couch her legs pulled up under her, while Mason pulled the arm chair closer to the couch so that the three of them were within touching distance, and gently took her hand inside his big, warm one.

"So yesterday we ended with you running away from

the foster home. Why don't you take it from there?" Dawn said gently.

Michelle nodded and dropped her head, her hair forming a curtain that Dawn wanted nothing more than to push away so she could watch those beautiful expressive chocolate brown eyes. She resisted the temptation knowing that Michelle would look at them in her own time.

"I ran away. After being on the streets for a few weeks I came across a carnival. You know rides and games; all that stuff. I had never been to a fair; the lights, the action, it attracted me like nothing I'd ever seen before. I was hungry, so hungry. If you've never lived on the streets you can't understand the hunger. But I ignored it and wandered around a place that seemed like magic. An enchanted village where real life never invaded." Michelle paused, lost in thought. Dawn had had the unpleasant experience of meeting a few carnies in her time. They were a breed apart from anything she'd ever seen before. Even though the majority of them were human, the ones she had met didn't seem right. She refocused on Michelle.

"What happened at the carnival?"

"For a while the sights and energy of the carnival distracted me, but when the hunger returned it overwhelmed me. It ate at me, my head spun and all I could see, all I could smell, was food. Cotton candy hanging in bags from the edges of carts, hot dogs wrapped in tin foil and just sitting there on counters. But I had no money.

Finally after hours of being there I couldn't resist and thinking myself so slick I grabbed a hot dog and tucked myself into an alley way between the merry go round and a water game. I gorged myself on that hot dog and still chewed it when they found me." Michelle paused, a catch in her voice foretelling the horrors that were about to come.

"Two men, big burly men, came and grabbed me. I don't remember much of what they said besides they knew I'd stolen the hot dog and they were taking me to the authorities. I was so terribly afraid." She caught her lower lip between her teeth and looked from Dawn to Mason. "I'm not a thief. Hunger took my sense of right and wrong, I couldn't think of anything besides filling the hole in my belly."

"We believe you." Mason said quietly to which Dawn nodded her agreement.

"I thought they were going to call the police but it turned out the authority they had called was the owner of the carnival." Her voice died off and a flash of fear came from Michelle so strong it nearly rocked Dawn off her axis. This owner must be the source of all her fears and pain. She passed the emotions on to Mason and worked on sending out calming energy to Michelle. She watched as Michelle seemed to straighten up and breathe easier.

"Phelon." She muttered. "I waited in this tiny trailer, his office for a long time, with one of the brutes standing by the door to make sure I didn't escape. When Phelon came in he sat at his desk and stared at me for a long time. I tried to apologize but he stared at me as though he didn't hear a word I said. I remember this tingling inside my head. My entire body vibrated with something weird which I ignored and did my sixteen year old best to leave. Finally he spoke. His voice silkier, smoother than I would have expected, almost sing-songy. He said that I now belonged to the carnival. I had to work off the theft and if I didn't they would call the cops and send me to juvenile detention."

She looked up; a fierceness in her eyes that made Dawn see the woman she could become with love and care. "I didn't believe him. I wasn't that stupid to think that because I stole a damned hot dog that I would go to jail or become property or whatever he implied. But I had nowhere else to go and no one else to turn to so I thought I would stay for a little while and pay them back before running away again."

The emotions flooding the room were full of self-recrimination and regrets and using the ability that she had been born with Dawn experienced them then passed them onto Mason. She waited in silence knowing that she couldn't push right now, Michelle needed a moment to collect herself before continuing.

"I stayed in a tiny trailer, no bigger than the bedroom of this cottage. Misery became my companion, but I owed them so I worked the rides for Phelon, not complaining because I got fed regularly. The fair travelled and I with it.

The oddness started almost right away, I would awaken so weakened I couldn't move. So tired I had no thoughts; just barely alive. No one bothered me but I became weary of everything. At the end of a month I decided I had had enough and I needed to leave. Phelon had always left a bad taste in my mouth. Even in my naiveté I knew there was something off about him so I decided to slip away in the middle of the night." Again she paused and Dawn knew they were getting to the heart of the story, the emotions, the energy swirling around Michelle grew thicker and more intense. She sent out good clean energy for Michelle to draw on, as she could see the petite woman growing more and weaker.

"I don't know if I should tell you anymore." She whispered. "I don't want to put you in danger, and I can still walk away without you knowing too much."

"You need to tell us." Mason grumbled softly. "We can and will protect you. We can and will heal you. Your soul needs you to talk. To get this story off your chest so that you can move beyond it. We need you to tell it so that we know what we are up against to help you heal."

Michelle locked eyes with Mason, the first time she'd looked at him closely without recoiling in fear and Dawn silently cheered. The healing had already helped, both what they were doing and Michelle telling the story had already began to stitch her back together. They stared at each other for long moments as the tension, the energy in the air that signaled their attraction for one another swirled around them. Michelle fought it but Dawn could still smell it as easily as she could breathe.

"Okay." Michelle took another deep breath. "So I gathered up my pitiful belongings and snuck out of the trailer after the carnival had shut down for the night. We were in Stratford, Ontario and set to leave in the morning. I thought if they couldn't find me they'd move on. I snuck out of the grounds and into the nearby forest. I thought for a few minutes I'd gotten away. I was wrong. I went around a tree and saw Phelon, with five of his henchman, standing there waiting for me. He asked where I was going. I told him that I had worked off my debt and needed to be moving on. He laughed. I'll never forget the sound of his laughter, it echoed through the trees and rang in my ears. He assured me I would never leave his carnival that I belonged to him. Two of the burly men grabbed my arms to prevent me from running." Dawn shivered she could see a younger version of Michelle struggling to escape, on her own surrounded by evil men older, and stronger than she had been. She shook off the vision as Michelle continued to speak. "I didn't understand a lot of what he said at the time. Mostly that he'd gone too easy on me and he needed to see if he could raise my levels. He stepped closer and said some words in a foreign language and I could see this blue cloud of sorts being drawn from inside me, coming out my mouth like smoke. He inhaled it, and seemed to grow stronger. By the time he finished I could barely stand, it felt like he'd sucked me dry. He leaned over and whispered, 'now we'll see how much we can fill up that battery.' He motioned to his men and they started punching me. I fell to the ground and they kicked and hit me for what seemed like hours, all the while I could sense this connection, this link between Phelon and me. He took all the energy I had, a stream of blue smoke pouring from inside me and going into him."

Dawn saw Mason stiffen up in anger that he quickly suppressed as Michelle continued. "Finally they stopped. I don't think he ever intended to have them kill me, I think he wanted to see how much I could take. How far he could go. I lay on the ground in more pain than I had ever experienced and he knelt beside me. He said that I had done well. He grinned with pleasure at the results of his experiment. But I had tried to run away and that was a no no. So I needed to be punished."

Dawn forced a growl down at the panic in Michelle's voice. She tamped down her own emotions and continued to send her the soothing energy she needed. She wanted nothing more than to rip that P.O.S to pieces with her claws to make him pay for hurting Michelle. However she also knew Michelle needed her comfort and not the righteous anger that coursed through her.

Michelle continued. "They punished me all right. They raped me." Her voice was harsh. "All five of them while Phelon watched. One after the other. I screamed until I had no voice left but they didn't care, it didn't stop anything. The worst part; the link still bound us together mentally, and while they hurt me through that connection between us I could feel Phelon's excitement. I knew how much the scene turned him on, it layered another torture on top of everything else I'd already experienced. And when they were finished he crawled up to me and swore that if I ever tried to escape again he would make sure next time they hurt me even more."

Tears leaked down Michelle's face as she relived the moments of her worst torment. She looked so tiny and frail on the couch that Dawn had to resist pulling her into her arms and taking the pain away. Instead she let Mason feed her good energy, let him take that painful memory and the energy surrounding it and strain it down, making it fade.

"How long ago did this happen?" Dawn asked quietly.

"Eight years." Michelle mumbled. "They kept me in a locked trailer for eight long years, with nothing but books and television. Phelon would come and drain me every couple of days. The beatings once a month or so. Very rarely did they touch my face, Phelon wanted to look at me and he couldn't with my face bruised and broken. He said all the time I belonged to him, like a little doll to take out and play with whenever he wanted. The beatings were bad, but my nightmares are still the way Phelon would look at me as his henchmen worked me over. As though I was nothing, a possession. Less than human." Dawn knew the shock on her face mirrored the look on Mason's. Michelle didn't appear to notice as she spoke again. "They didn't..." her voice broke again, "rape me again. They didn't need to.

I became totally compliant, under their utter control. A toy they could play with whenever they wanted. Whenever and however they wanted."

"Eventually they got complacent about locking me up, especially after a beating, since I appeared so weakened by the draining and the pain that they were less cautious than they should have been. Last week I could see the St. Lawrence River from the tiny window in my trailer, we were in Brockville. Phelon needed extra power for something new he planned for the show. So they worked me over. They beat me as bad as they had that first time and left me laying there, bleeding and so weak I thought I would die. I escaped before they realized they hadn't locked the door. I knew I had no strength and they would come after me. I didn't care if I died I knew I couldn't do it again. Not ever again. So I stumbled to the end of the dock and jumped into the water. Prepared to die rather than go back to that non-existent life I had been enduring."

She refused to make eye contact as she whispered. "And here I am. Don't think he won't come for me. No matter how safe you think it is here, he'll find me. I am too useful to him." She paused and looked at her lap, where her fingers fidgeted nervously. "Now you know. You can see how broken I am. Please let me go before something happens and one of you gets hurt."

Dawn could barely speak through the anger and sorrow but she reached out and gently took Michelle's hand in her own. "We aren't going anywhere." Her voice broke.

43

"You may have been hurt by the past," Mason spoke as well also reaching out slowly for Michelle's other hand, his voice low but firm. "And you may have been damaged by what happened to you. But you are not broken. Together we will repair the damage done to you. We will defeat the shadows from your past and make sure nothing ever comes close to hurting you in the future." Dawn knew how sincere his words were, she knew the depth of his emotions. A flush of hope whirled through her, when for the first time since meeting Michelle she let Mason touch her without flinching away.

She watched as Mason skillfully took the negative energies produced by the telling of the tale and spun it into softer edges and positive energy and fed it back to Michelle. Who had noticeably perked up with the renewed energy. She aided as much as possible but admired the skill that Mason demonstrated while he worked.

"How do you feel now?" She asked.

Michelle seemed to consider the question before answering. "Better. Certainly not one hundred percent yet but better than this morning. I am pretty tired though." She turned to include both of them in her beaming look.

"Tired is a good sign." Dawn assured her. "While your energy levels are healing your body is also healing. And it needs sleep to repair the damage done to you. A nap before we go for dinner is a good idea."

Michelle barely restrained a huge yawn before nodding

sheepishly. She stood and carefully made her way back to the bedroom.

~~~

As soon as the door closed behind her Mason jumped to his feet and began pacing looking like a caged tiger. His anger came off in waves.

"Mason." Dawn spoke quietly. "You need to calm down."

"I cannot believe what she lived through." In his mind's eye he kept seeing the scene she had described. The tiny trailer she had been held captive in for eight long years. How could someone be so evil, so inhumane to treat a beautiful woman like Michelle like that? Mason wanted to rip that Phelon to tiny pieces after pummeling him until the vile, bitter taste in his mouth disappeared.

"I know." Dawn spoke her voice quiet and full of conviction. "She is strong. We will all get through this. She's known nothing but pain, both physical and mental her whole life. We will show her love and compassion and help her."

Mason tried to breathe but bile kept choking him.

45

Intellectually he knew what Dawn said made sense his heart physically ached for how badly their soul mate had been treated. Finally he shoved a hand through his hair leaving it messy and unkempt looking. While he still held deep reservations and concerns regarding his possible involvement with Michelle he couldn't stand her pain. The things she had suffered shook him to his core.

While she spoke it had been all he could do not to jump up and hold her in his arms forever. To take care of her like no one in her life ever had, to use his arms and his body to protect and cherish the tiny beautiful woman who had come to mean so much more to him than he could have anticipated. He had resisted the temptation with an iron will that would rival Thors hammer, but it had been a close call.

"Have you figured out what she is yet?" He asked trying to distract himself from the anger that took his entire being.

"I've never seen anything like her. But I believe she might be the equivalent to a battery. Her energy fills quicker than any human I've known and even as you were pulling the energy from her she still had more to give." Mason nodded, Dawn's assessment matched his own.

Frowning he said. "I agree. The problem is, if she is an inexhaustible source or energy, this Phelon will never give up on getting her back. Not that we are going to let him touch her ever again. But it sounds as though he is a

46

warlock, and a treat like Michelle would be irresistible, she would allow him to cast unending spells without ever having to use his own energies."

Finally having distracted himself from the fury that bubbled below the surface Mason sat back down. "We are going to have to be extra careful with her. Make sure absolutely nothing gets to her."

Dawn nodded and they fell into silence each of them lost in their own thoughts. A small noise from the doorway signaled Michelle's return. She stood looking at the ground, nervousness leaching off her in droves. She fidgeted with the hem of her shirt and shuffled her feet.

"Is everything okay, Solotke?" Mason asked forcing his heartbeat to slow as he stared at the stunning creature who had suffered so much.

She shook her head, her pitch black hair swaying with the movement. "I hoped, that is to say...I wondered if...I wanted..." She groaned. "Damn it. This shouldn't be so difficult." Squaring her shoulders she looked up at the two of them. "I'm not exactly scared, more uneasy and I hoped you might come hold me while I fell asleep. I am not ready for anything else but I would like to try being held."

His heart jumped into his throat with joy. She had reached out to them, and no matter how much fear overwhelmed her she had forced her way through it to ask for the comfort they were more than happy to give. He forced the pleasure back, she might only want Dawn, after the way men had treated her in the past Mason knew he had a lot of ground to make up.

Dawn stood. "I would like nothing more than to give you comfort. To hold you and keep you safe even in sleep." Her voice broke with raw emotion as she moved towards Michelle.

Michelle smiled lightly at Dawn and then looked past her, making eye contact with Mason. "You too?" Her voice squeaked and nerves came off her in waves.

"It would be my honor and privilege." Mason shot to his feet and moved to the doorway with the other two. They stepped into the room and Michelle fidgeted nervously as though now unsure how to proceed.

"How about you hop up in the center and we'll spoon you?" Dawn asked.

Michelle nodded and climbed fully dressed onto the bed. Mason had never been overly fond of yoga pants but seeing them on Michelle's dainty little body sent his libido into overdrive. He forced the emotions to the side and waited while Michelle got comfortable in the middle of the king sized bed, her tiny body dwarfed as she lay on her back.

He went to one side and sat on the edge reaching out and taking her hand as he spoke. "I want you to promise me if anything scares you, or makes you uncomfortable you tell me right away and I will leave or stop." He vowed inside his brain even if it killed him to stop he would never hurt her. She nodded timidly and Mason stretched out beside her.

He lay on his side facing her, feeling as though he had come home for the first time in his life. He still held her hand in his, as he looked at her face relaxing slightly. The bed dipped as Dawn climbed in on the opposite side and mirrored Mason's position. They were close enough to hold hands but not mauling her and Michelle breathed a sigh.

"That's better." She murmured sleepily.

Mason watched as her eyes slowed drooped, closing and opening several times each time taking longer until she gave in to the sleep that she so desperately needed. He stared at her for quite a while, memorizing the planes and angles of her face. The line of her neck, all the things that made her Michelle.

Finally comfortable with the one woman made for him Mason allowed sleep to take him.

~~~

*M*ichelle smiled up at Mason as he brought her a plate overflowing with battered mushrooms. He had discovered that they were her favorite and had somehow managed to find some to make for her. The last three days had been therapeutic, every day the three of them worked on her energy levels followed by a walk through the forest that surrounded the retreat. Calia had had daily physical healing sessions with her timed around her busy schedule running the retreat.

They had made tentative forays into talking with the other guests. They were a singularly interesting bunch of people. All artists in varying states of their careers. Mika a writer housed in cabin 3 struggled with finishing her manuscript. Boston was a musician who fiddled with his guitar whenever he spoke. Cathy had the cabin next to the big house where Michelle was staying and she painted beautiful landscapes with watercolors. Overall the retreat had a calm but creative vibe that relaxed Michelle. She still worried about Phelon finding her but Calia assured her the land was magically attuned to her and would let her know if anyone meaning harm to her or the other guests would be discovered immediately. She was safe.

The memories of her attack and imprisonment were fading to a dull ache rather than the immediate horrifying pain that they had been. She knew that without the help of both Mason and Dawn that she wouldn't be nearly as healed as she seemed to be now, that the energy and memory healing they were doing had aided her in ways she would never be able to repay them for. For what seemed like the first time in forever she thought of herself as an actual human being and less like a shell.

Each night Dawn and Mason held her as she slept. The dreams that had haunted her for the last eight years seemed to have disappeared. They had progressed from holding hands to spooning each other. Michelle had never felt so decadent, so cared for; she kept pinching herself to see if her imagination had created this entire episode and she would awaken to be stuck in the trailer, her nostrils filled with the overwhelming scent of rancid popcorn and despair. Much to her amazement she had yet to discover this wasn't real.

It had been a lovely, healing interlude from real life. She still hadn't been convinced about this whole mate business, the only person to complete these two generous and stunning creatures who were her caregivers. She figured they would tire soon of her endless needs and damage but until then she took the time to learn to live without fear and to learn that not all men were horrible. She had come to trust them, to believe they wanted to keep her safe. The Cubus had never made a further move on her, they held her at night, they talked and laughed with her, in short they were perfect. They had a deep connection and affection that both thrilled and terrified Michelle. She had learned more about the Cubus and the world she now found herself embroiled in.

The first night they had spent holding her hands she had only been looking for comfort. Recently however she found herself longing for more. Each night she became more aware of their bodies close to hers in the bed and lust stirred deep inside her. She wasn't stupid, she had watched

51

television and read a lot of books over the years, and Michelle knew that her emotions were normal, she had however never expected to experience them herself. To yearn for a man, and a woman with all her being. To want to touch and be touched. To need them to kiss her and show her that she existed as a real person and not some shadow forever fated to be used and alone. It overwhelmed her and Michelle had no idea how to take things to the next level. She also fought against the terror of what the next level would be. Prior to being kidnapped she had made it to second base with a boy in her class. Her extremely limited sexual experience even before the experience in the forest worried her. Her constant fear of disappointing them threatened to overwhelm her. That they would discover how badly scarred and inept she would always be. She feared she would never be normal.

She knew Phelon would be coming for her, and soon the dream had to end. That thought sent a blast of cold fear through her. She didn't want it to end, but if she had learned one thing her life she had learned that she had no one else to rely on. Each day her physical strength returned, the healing Calia performed on her had taken her horrific looking bruises and faded them until they were barely visible. She could go to dinner without the other guests staring at her.

"Michelle? Are you going to eat those or just stare at them?" Mason's soft voice jolted Michelle and she blushed at being caught woolgathering.

"Sorry. I was lost in thought." She murmured and popped a mushroom into her mouth closing her eyes at the deep fried bliss that rushed through her. She opened her eyes and found Mason staring at her mouth with intensity in his eyes. She knew he seemed to find her attractive, he told her often enough and at night with him spooning her body his erection had pressed into her back more than once. It gave her a heady sense of power and not a small amount of trepidation. She swallowed the mushroom, momentarily forgetting what she ate in favor of the look in Mason's eyes.

He cleared his throat. "So what is the plan for tonight, Solotke?"

"I am not sure." She answered. "Do you have any ideas?"

He nodded. "Dawn and I were thinking," At the mention of her name another shot of lust spread through Michelle's body which she ignored to focus on Mason's words. "It might do you good to go to the waterfall." At Michelle's raised eyebrow Mason elaborated. "Ray is a Nymph who helped Calia pull the water from a warm spring deep in the earth so it is just like being in a hot tub. A natural hot tub surrounded by forests. We were wondering if you wanted to go there and take a swim. The waters are healing and will help to aid in removing your physical aches."

"That sounds nice." Michelle answered, images

rushing through her brain of how they would look bathed in moonlight with the water of a hot spring sliding across their skin and she had to forcibly swallow again. Quickly she changed the subject. "I've been meaning to ask, you always call me Solotke. What does it mean? Why do you call me that?"

Mason looked down as embarrassment flashed across his face momentarily. Clearing his throat he spoke. "As a baby my family immigrated to America from the Ukraine. My parents never took the life we found here for granted. They were educated folks and wanted to help other new Americans so my mother worked as a translator for Ukrainian immigrants. Unfortunately, I didn't learn much of the language; too busy being a kid and trying to fit in. A hard enough chore when you aren't human to begin with, but I did learn that Solotke meant 'sweet'. It's a term of endearment that seemed right for you."

Michelle didn't know what to say about the term of endearment so she munched lightly on the mushrooms.

"And how are your battered mushrooms?" Dawn walked up beside them a smile lighting her face.

"Delicious." Michelle grinned back and pushed the plate towards her. "Would you like to try one?"

"Not for me." Dawn shivered. "I'm not crazy about mushrooms. They are grown in shit. I can't get past that." Michelle laughed.

"Not that long ago I really didn't care where food grew as long as I got some. I would have eaten the shit these grew in." Michelle grinned and took a big bite of the sizzling mushroom.

"I'm glad you are starting to be able to joke about some things." Mason leaned forward, his big body radiating relief.

"Anyway." Dawn pulled up a chair and sat so close that the heat coming off her body warmed Michelle. "Calia wants to meet with us after we eat. Ray just came in and I think he has some news."

A stab of nerves rushed through her system. The muscled Ray had been looking into Phelon and the carnival. Whether her nerves were at the thought of talking about the carnival or facing the Nymph, she didn't know.

Suddenly the mushrooms looked like cardboard and Michelle knew she couldn't eat any more. Dawn covered one hand and whispered. "It will be okay."

"Please don't worry." Mason gently took the other hand. "We'll be there with you and no harm will come to you."

Michelle nodded woodenly. "Let's get this over with." She stood, her chair making a scraping noise on the floor. Mason and Dawn flanked her each holding a hand as they moved to the small office building at the back of the pavilion that Calia called her headquarters.

Michelle tried to avoid thinking about what they were going to find out by instead focusing on the two Cubus beside her.

She knew with her rational brain that she should be running from this retreat as fast as possible. After all she shared her bed with two creatures of the night. Ones that folk tales told about how Succubus and Incubus sucked the souls from people while they slept, leading to their deaths. No matter how often rational brain screamed at her, Michelle couldn't bring herself to leave. Or even to be scared any longer. She knew in her heart that Dawn and Mason would never hurt her.

Now looking sideways at first Mason and then Dawn, Michelle's smiled lightly. Who would have ever thought that she would be here? Free and choosing to hang out with two beautiful para creatures who seemed to want her as much as she wanted them.

The door swung open and Calia waved them in with a smile. She sat at a crowded desk with Ray beside her, a file folder dwarfed in his big hand. Although he wasn't tall he made even Mason look like a newbie at physical training and Michelle appeared to be a child (a lazy and overweight child at that) next to him.

Michelle forced herself not to shrink away as Ray's bright green eyes turned to her. "Michelle. You're looking much better."

She nodded and didn't speak. She knew her fears were

irrational but at that exact moment she couldn't have spoken if her hair caught on fire. Both Mason and Dawn reached for her hands as though they were as distressed as she, which given their powers Michelle figured they were. A calming coolness echoed through her that she knew came from them and she took advantage of it as she finally managed a deep breath.

"Alright Ray, what have you learned?" Dawn asked squeezing Michelle's hand comfortingly.

Ray flipped open the folder and quickly scanned its contents as though familiarizing himself with the information contained. "I put out some feelers looking for anything on this carnival, or Phelon. It looks as though the Hidden Protection Collective, the HPC have been investigating them before I started. It took a little while to get them to give up what they had," Ray grinned ferally, "but I managed to convince them. After all it does little to no good being the mayor if I can't call in a favour when needed."

"Phelon Masters is his name. He is a warlock who according to the HPC has much more power than he should. He ran his families carnival with mediocre success for years until about seven years ago when it started to flourish. His unparalleled success brought the attention of the HPC a few years ago. The good news is that they raided the fair last week, around the time of your escape." He nodded towards Michelle. "It is now out of commission. The bad news is that Phelon wasn't there when the raid took place.

No one has seen him since then." Michelle tensed up, fear shooting through her system. "Don't worry too much. The land here protects its people. It will notify Calia if there are any problems. I am keeping an eye out in town and all the artists that come to Whispering Winds are thoroughly vetted before being allowed on the property. Calia takes her security seriously." He nodded at Calia who grinned at his compliment. "With Dawn and Mason's protection you are as safe as possible at Whispering Winds."

Michelle flushed embarrassed at Ray being able to read her so easily. "It's okay." Mason murmured softly.

"Anyways I wanted you to know that there is a HPC wide warrant out for his arrest and I've called a friend on the local force, he will eventually want to talk with you. He is also a Warlock who hopefully will be able to remove the mental hooks Phelon put in your mind. For now I've told him you are healing and cannot be disturbed." Ray smiled gently at Michelle. "We will take care of you." His voice as gentle as she had ever heard it. "Now you guys go get on with the healing and let us deal with the HPC and carnival on your behalf."

"Thank you." Mason and Dawn stood pulling lightly on Michelle until she joined them.

She turned back to Ray and forced her fear down saying in a soft voice. "I am sorry to be such a trouble to you. But I thank you for helping me when you had no reason to."

Ray stayed seated and smiled gently. "Don't thank me. Just get better."

They exited the office and Dawn drove them back to the cottage in a golf cart. Each cottage was given a solar powered cart to get around the property. Calia allowed no fossil fueled vehicles on her property. She had over 30 acres of forested property that had been converted into the Whispering Winds Artist Retreat a few years ago. The property had a small parking lot at the edge where guests left their vehicles when they arrived down that gravel road, they were checked in and taken to their cabins. Each of the seven cabins on the property was a single room building, rustic without being primitive. The retreat itself was beauty personified. Surrounded by forest on three sides and the St. Lawrence river on the fourth they had trails to walk, views to die for and nature filling every moment of every day. An escape that allowed artists to reconnect with themselves. To sequester and focus on their work. Michelle watched the trees slip by, lost in thought.

The people she had met since coming to Whispering Winds had nearly restored her faith in others. Even before being kidnapped she had been shown so little care and affection, so little love that in some ways this place and its occupants were overwhelming. She really didn't know how it could possibly be that she got so lucky to be found and brought here, but Michelle knew without a doubt that she wouldn't have survived without it.

~~~

*M*ason ran a hand through his shaggy hair, frustration evident on his face. He never let this side of him show with Michelle present, but damn the woman drove him to distraction. He could hardly function for wanting her so bad, but as Dawn and he had discussed she had to come to them herself. Being Incubus he could taste the sexual energy that came off her in waves and it drove him mad. He knew with his brain that she had to take the lead and make the first move. Even if it took years to have her be comfortable with them, he would do it. He would rather die than be the cause of any fear in Michelle's sweet heart. He knew it with his head; his body hated the wait.

Two days ago they noticed a jump in her self-confidence when Calia brought her a selection of clothes that weren't cast offs. She had very sweetly run into town with Dell, her friend, and grabbed a bunch of clothes for Michelle to keep. She swore it would help, and while Mason didn't understand it, it certainly did seem to perk Michelle up. She had teared up and thanked Calia so profusely that Mason wished for a moment he had thought of it. Calia had, with her usual aplomb, brushed off the thanks saying that every girl deserved to have a wardrobe of her own and she knew that Dawn's clothes would be too big.

Mason looked towards the bedroom. Michelle had been overwhelmed and tired by talking to Ray and when they had returned to the cottage she had escaped to lay down for a bit. If he opened his senses he knew he would feel the steady driftless energy of her sleeping.

Dawn sprawled comfortably on the easy chair, her long legs hanging over the plush arm, a book in her hand as she too waited for Michelle. She held the book easily but her eyes kept darting to the bedroom as though she too watched for Michelle. It amazed Mason how quickly she had become indispensable to them. She had crept into their hearts, silently and without effort until Mason knew he wouldn't survive if she left them.

An unheard of feat for an Incubus, who lived and breathed sexual energy, to have a mate become so ingrained to his heart that he couldn't function without her, before they'd even had sex. He needed her, like a tree needed sunlight, and his body hummed in anticipation whenever she happened to be near. His shock had nearly overwhelmed him when he discovered someone like her existed, someone who could be a soul mate to him and Dawn. As much as he ached with wanting her, he also knew that they had forever and he wouldn't rush the decision.

The door opened and Mason's breath caught in his throat. Michelle stepped through uncertainty in her every step. She stood in the doorway, eyes downcast and fidgeting with the hem of her t-shirt.

"What's wrong Solotke?" Mason stood and moved towards her with Dawn matching his stride.

"I wanted to ask you something." She whispered, her voice barely audible.

"Anything." Dawn sounded firm and no nonsense. She had asserted over and over that Michelle could say anything, ask anything and they would answer honestly. So far Michelle had been pretty stingy with her questions, clearly not wanting to rock the boat.

Mason's heart leapt into his throat as he watched Michelle's almond shaped chocolate brown eyes furrow as though she tried to find the words. He stayed silent letting Michelle find her wording without interference.

"You know that I haven't lived the most normal of lives. And while this week has been an idyllic escape from the reality that is my existence, I know it can't last. Sooner or later Phelon will find me, or I'll have to return to real life and oh I don't know, find a job. Maybe graduate from high school. See if a missing person report had ever been placed on me. What I'm saying is soon I'll have to start real life."

She paused and Mason fought to keep breathing, it sounded like the standard 'it's not you, it's me' speech, in preparation of leaving them. He held still and kept his mouth shut.

"I've never..." Michelle visibly inhaled. "I've never chosen to be with anyone. Every choice in my life has been taken away from me, including sex. I don't want that now. I want to choose to be with you. To try to be a normal person for once, to accept myself as a sexual being. I don't know how this will work with three people." She blushed furiously. "My emotions are tipping the scale, I never thought I would experience the emotions that you two have evoked in me. Lust and attraction were foreign concepts and now, thanks to you I have experienced them. I'm not sure if I am explaining myself properly or if I am just blubbering here, but I now know that I need to try. I can't promise I won't screw up. Or freak out, however I want to try."

Silence fell over the room as Mason fought the urge to sweep Michelle into his arms and kiss her luscious mouth until the insecurity in her eyes faded. He tamped down his primal urges with a willpower he didn't know he possessed.

Michelle spoke again, her voice even softer. "If you still want to, that is."

"Of course we want to." Dawn growled. "We want nothing more. We have wanted nothing more for the last four days, I am fighting down the urge to throw you over my shoulder and take you immediately to bed." Mason nodded in agreement, still unable to speak. Michelle looked up shock in her eyes.

"Oh, okay then." She smiled shyly. "So how does this work? I don't know what to do."

"Don't worry. We'll take it as it goes." Dawn moved

slowly towards Michelle.

"And if anything scares you, or if something isn't right, you just say so and everything stops." Mason finally found his voice. "I don't care if it kills me, I will stop before I do anything that scares you."

~~~

*M*ichelle tried to stop her heart from beating out of her chest. Nerves combined with an unknown excitement at the same time until she thought she would jitter out of her skin. She looked back and forth between Dawn and Mason, her heartbeat ratcheting up a notch.

They moved towards her with caution evident in every step, as though Michelle had become a frightened deer who would run away at the slightest noise. Dawn reached her first, and ran her long, graceful fingers up Michelle's arm causing a round of goosebumps to rush over her skin.

Dawn leaned in and softly placed her perfectly shaped lips against Michelle's. Her hands framed Michelle's face as her lips softly plucked at Michelle's. Michelle's lips opened slowly as a sensation of flying overwhelmed her and she kissed this sensual woman back, allowing her access to the cavern of her mouth. They kissed for long moments, slowly getting to know one another. Their tongues sliding against each other in a sensual dance of restraint and desire. Dawn relaxed Michelle with little licks and nips teasing her tongue back and forth until Michelle could barely breathe.

They finally pulled away and Michelle could read the lust in Dawn's eyes as she released Michelle's hair. Mason stood beside Michelle and waited until she looked up at him then he softly touched her hair, brushing it back off her cheek.

"So beautiful." He whispered and with his fingertips touching her angular cheekbone he too kissed her. The only parts of their bodies that touched were their lips and his fingers as they fluttered over the skin of her face. He too moved slowly and gently allowing Michelle the time to become accustomed to his scent, his essence.

She wrinkled her brow as she returned the kiss opening her lips to take the first step and taste him. She would have never expected that kissing two people could be so different. He smelt different, muskier and tasted mintier. His lips were firmer and although gentleness seeped out of him in waves, she knew he restrained himself. He vibrated power and strength and with a shock Michelle realized her panties were getting damp.

Slowly he pulled away, looking deep into her eyes. "Okay?" He asked to which Michelle nodded and with a bravery she didn't know she possessed she took his hand. Together the three of them walked into the bedroom and once inside Michelle turned to them, uncertainty again in her eyes.

Mason slowly ran his hands up and down her arms, relaxing her slightly as his warm touch made tingles run through her body. He stepped up closer to Michelle who was dwarfed by the sheer size of him. She looked up at him and as he leaned down to lock his lips to hers she forgot all about the difference in their heights. She found herself leaning into the kiss, savoring each moment, each stolen breath, her body longing for more. He worked his way along her cheekbone placing small kisses as he traced her face with his lips.

Michelle closed her eyes and lost herself in the sensations. She could sense Dawn behind her, touching her hair and murmuring comforting nothings. Her hands floated down her back and teased the skin under the hem of her t-shirt. Michelle's stomach trembled as she let her head fall back to rest on Dawn's shoulder. Mason worked his soft lips across her neck leaving a trail of shivering hot flesh.

He licked a path up her jugular to the edge of her ear. "Let us worship you." He whispered and then as she sighed he sucked the bud of her earlobe into his mouth and suckled gently.

Dawn's arms surrounded Michelle holding her and caressing her skin lightly keeping her on edge. Somehow they made it to the bed and Michelle opened her eyes to meet Mason's lust filled ones.

"Are you okay with us undressing you?" Dawn asked softly. Michelle unable to speak, nodded her agreement. Four hands reached below her shirt and caressing their way lightly up, touching her ribs and skirting the underside of her heaving breasts. Teasing, they gently pulled the t-shirt over her head and dropped it to the ground.

A simultaneous groan erupted from both Dawn and Mason as they moved closer. Michelle kept her eyes closed not wanting to ruin the moment with a vision of herself. She fought the urge to cover up, how could she stand topless next to these two perfect creatures?

"Hey." Mason's voice cut through her thoughts. "No negativity. You are beautiful."

"Exquisite." Dawn agreed pressing into her from behind. Every curve of her body molded to Michelle's and she inhaled sharply at the sensation. Sleeping next to them for the last few nights she had inadvertently learned their bodies but that had a very different connotation than them touching her intimately and with intent.

Slowly she opened her eyes and read the lust on Mason's face as he regarded her body and her nipples tightened into painful points. She turned her head and caught Dawn's lips in a kiss that pushed any remaining doubt from her mind. Fingers skimmed her breasts plucking at her nipples while others lightly touched her entire upper body until Michelle found herself panting. A soft touch at her waist line and she opened her eyes to see Mason on his knees in front of her, his hands spanning her waist gently. Their eyes connected and with Dawn pressed comfortingly into her from behind he gently popped open the button to her jeans. The zipper seemed unusually loud in the room filled only with their breathing.

Michelle took a deep breath and stepped away, ignoring the flash of concern in their eyes. As much as she loved what they were doing she needed to take some control. Everything in her life had been done to her, this, being with them, was one thing she wanted to choose herself. To show her choice without doubt. She had to take some initiative in their love making.

She slowly peeled her jeans down her legs, taking the soft cotton panties with them and then stepped out of them, standing naked in front of someone for the first time. Her dark skin flushed with lust and some inevitable embarrassment, but she met their eyes steadily.

"Michelle." Dawn groaned.

"Dear God, you are stunning." Mason added before they pulled her back into their embrace and settled her comfortably on the bed. Dawn knelt on one side of her and Mason on the other, and their fingers stroked her skin, lips skimmed her face and neck until Michelle thought she would explode from the emotions. A dampness between her thighs signaled her passion as they continued to caress her.

Slowly working their way down her arms until they kissed her fingertips, both Dawn and Mason stood. First Dawn moved to the foot of the bed. "Look at me, sweetheart."

Michelle hungrily stared at the beautiful woman as she, without artifice, removed her pants revealing a tiny bright pink thong. Her fingers slowly undid the buttons on her shirt allowing it to fall open exposing a matching bra. Michelle's heart nearly stopped as she took in the perfect pale skin, and tiny waist curving gently to narrow hips. She dropped her shoulders and the shirt slid down her arms to hit the floor. The bra and thong followed suit quickly and without wasting time.

Michelle took a moment to commit the memory of Dawn's beauty to her mind. Michelle had dark reddish skin compared with the almost translucent skin of Dawns. Her nipples were turgid peaks, a light pink tip on top of small high breasts. Michelle fought a shock at Dawn's hairless womanhood, she'd heard of it but never seen or tried it herself. Michelle's legs were well shaped but short and Dawn's were long and gleamed in the faint light in the room.

"You are..." Michelle couldn't find words as she stared at this unbelievable woman who stood before her. She shook her head, her senses overwhelmed.

Dawn smiled gently and climbed onto the bed, looking faintly feline as she slithered up Michelle's body. Her buzz cut only emphasized the wide blue eyes that captured Michelle's sight and captivated her until she couldn't look away.

Finally they were eye to eye and lip to lip, nothing else touching as Dawn hovered above her with passion in her eyes. Her lips softly brushed against Michelle's once again, and she stretched her neck trying to ease some of the desire within her, she thrust a tongue into Dawn's mouth and let all her lust show in the kiss. Dawn met her immediately with an eagerness of her own and their tongues tangled, in an intimate getting to know one another ritual.

She pulled away and bit her lip as Dawn pressed her body against Michelle's. The smoothness, the warmth of another woman's breasts pressed against her own caused a lightening like ripple to flow through Michelle's entire being. Their nipples rubbed together, tightening Michelle's until she gasped with the eroticism. Dawn captured the gasp with her lips and for long moments they kissed their tongues sliding across one another, bodies pressed and arms tangled as they caressed each other.

With a small groan Dawn slid to the side and looked to the foot of the bed where Mason watched, his eyes glinting with restrained desire. Michelle pushed herself up on her elbows and looked down the length of her body to watch as he impatiently pulled his shirt over his head revealing a long torso with well-defined muscles, a hairless chest and washboard abs that had a small trail of hair leading below his waist. His strong hands moved to his shorts and quickly slipped them down to the floor stepping out of them. He waited long moments giving Michelle the time she needed to examine him. Her eyes swept over his body, starting at his feet. His legs were long and covered in a light sheen of blond hair that couldn't disguise the tan that he had. For the moment she skimmed over his pelvis, her heartbeat quickening but she ignored it instead looking at his wide chest and powerful arms. Memorizing each hard plane and surface. Finally she held her breath and followed the muscles down, taking a moment to check out his fabulous man v until she settled on his pelvis. His large member jutted out, bobbing towards the bed in a reflexive movement. Nestled in a bed of dark blond hair a bead of moisture clung to the tip making it appear to weep.

As Michelle watched, Mason shivered his whole body convulsing with longing. She grew faint and had to force herself to take a breath. Finally after looking at his body she looked back and met his eyes. A corner of his mouth quirked up in question. Michelle smiled back and Mason quickly climbed on the bed on the opposite side of Dawn.

He caught her lips in a kiss that stole her thoughts with its heat. This time Mason let his ardor loose showing her the passion he held by a firm leash. Hands caressed her and touched her breasts, her arms, her legs as Mason ravished her mouth and left her wanting so much more.

His lips trailed down her body and simultaneously with Dawn they each took a stiff peak in their mouths and suckled gently. Unable to hold back Michelle let voice to her pleasure, crying out their names as her head thrashed from side to side. Her hands drifted to their shoulders and running her finger nails lightly on their backs Michelle gave herself over to the emotions. Her thighs became drenched with a moisture that evidenced her arousal. They suckled and used their hands to knead her breasts until she gasped, incoherent with desire. Mason moaned lightly around her nipple and the vibrations jolted straight from her breast to the burning core of her.

She could feel them and their passion; both in her body and in her brain. She knew how much they wanted her and could sense them in the back of her mind. Knowing they were inside her mind and how unbelievably turned on they were only fueled Michelle's emotions further. She could easily separate the bits that were Dawn, her pure lust from Mason's harsh desire tinged with concern. She knew without thinking which thoughts and emotions were hers, and which were the others. Each had their own flavor, like separate voices. Unique and individual even though they were all in her mind.

Overwhelmed Michelle felt her body tighten and a release she didn't know could exist rippled through her entire body. She cried out with passionate abandon as she experienced her first orgasm. It rippled through her body giving life to the most incredible sensations, a tingling in all her extremities until Michelle thought she might pass out.

When she finally opened her eyes she found both

Mason and Dawn resting their heads on her stomach looking up at her as their fingers brushed gently over her sensitized skin, soft smiles on their faces. She smiled lightly back at them and whispered. "Wow."

"You are perfection." Mason whispered back, before he moved up her body and kissed her swollen lips once more. "Better than I could ever have hoped for." He murmured against her lips.

With some shifting he settled behind her with Michelle reclining against his strong body while his fingers continued to stroke her lightly, keeping her on the edge of desire. Meanwhile Dawn stroked her legs and stomach with gentle fingers. Michelle's shocked eyes shot open as her body started to respond again.

"Shall we continue?" Dawn's husky voice vibrated across her skin as she looked at Michelle who nodded in agreement. Dawn grinned and slid down her body until she rested on her elbows between Michelle's thighs. Her fingers stroked Michelle's skin, closer and closer to the core of her until Michelle found herself holding her breath every time and sighing in frustration when Dawn avoided touching her.

Mason stroked her upper arms and breasts gently, in time with Dawn's tender stroking, his arms holding her comfortably, giving her security and safety. From their minds Michelle sensed nothing but a longing to make her know how much they wanted her.

Finally after agonizingly erotic moments Dawn slid her fingers down her slit and Michelle found her hips thrusting towards her fingers. Using one hand Dawn parted Michelle's lips and stroked the length of her womanhood, her fingers circling the straining bundle of nerves. Michelle let out a groan and found herself unable to control her body as she pushed herself towards Dawn wanting more, but unsure about what she wanted.

Dawn chuckled, and whispered, "You need more don't you sweetheart?" Her breath whispering against Michelle's heated skin. Without waiting for an answer Dawn inhaled her scent deeply and lowered her head, tasting the core of her. She licked her from opening to clit, her tongue following the path her fingers had recently taken.

Dawn suckled at her clit, making little humming noises in the back of her throat that vibrated through Michelle's being. Michelle could feel herself getting impossibly wet, her juices flowing out as her body grew tighter still. Dawn slowly slipped a finger inside Michelle's channel and she cried out with the pleasure, as Dawn continued to work her nub of desire, alternately licking it lightly and sucking on it with more pressure bringing Michelle to the precipice and then changing her tactics until she calmed down, again and again. Her finger worked slowly inside Michelle keeping pace with her tongue and Michelle thought she would explode from the sensations.

Mason's fingers plucked at her nipples in time with Dawn's tongue and they were both crooning at her in wordless approval. Their emotions, their completion and happiness wrapped around Michelle bringing her once again to the very edge of arousal until she couldn't take it any longer and she cried out, "Please!" In a strangled voice.

Dawn's buzz cut tickled lightly between her legs, rubbed the overly sensitive skin of her thighs and drove Michelle ever higher. Another orgasm buzzed at the side of her brain, ready to explode. Dawn moaned and refocused her attention on Michelle's clit, sucking it between her lips firmly as her fingers slid along the inner wall of her vagina, finding her g-spot and igniting Michelle further as she stroked the pleasure point insistently.

Suddenly Michelle grasped Dawn's head and held her tight as she couldn't control herself and thrust her pelvis against Dawn's face with abandon. Mason pinched her nipples lightly, pulling the on tight tips which set Michelle off. She screamed, unable to hold back, her inner walls pulsing and pulling on Dawn's fingers, milking her as she came. In her mind Dawn roared with her own orgasm, and a warm wetness on her back told the tale of Mason finding his own release.

Her entire body tingled with aftershocks of pleasure as she fell into a boneless heap on the bed, she knew she would be unable to move even if the cottage burned around her. A half smile floated on her lips, and she knew she'd never forget this moment for as long as she lived.

Dawn climbed off the bed and slid into the bathroom

for a moment before returning with a cloth and the two of them gently cleaned up Michelle, wiping the sticky residue from her back and between her legs. They murmured softly to her, words that she couldn't focus on as she rode the wave of euphoria that still held her in its grasp.

Finally they cuddled in around her, surrounding her and protecting her as all three of them drifted off to sleep.

~~~

*D*awn grinned to herself, feeling like she'd won a gold medal at the Olympics, last night had been the best night of her life. Watching Michelle give herself up to the desires that Dawn knew swirled inside had been amazing.

She made her way through forest to the small sun dappled pasture where she had agreed to meet Michelle after meditation class given by Dell. It had been suggested by Calia that Michelle attend and Dawn had agreed. Breathing deeply and allowing oneself to relax in a mini meditation could be conducive to healing. She only hoped Michelle could let herself accept the class with an open mind. Her heart sped up as she drove the golf cart closer, in the distance she could see a number of people sitting on yoga mats facing the forest. Her eyes were immediately drawn to Michelle, her black hair blowing in the breeze with the sun kissing her face, she was a vision.

Taking a deep breath Dawn parked the cart and hopped out moving quietly towards the class, not wanting to disturb them. Dell looked up and acknowledged Dawn with a nod. Today she had restrained her blond hair in a long braid down her back. While Dell was a human, she was a friend to the Hidden and had known of their existence for many years as Calia's best friend. She waved towards Michelle with a wink.

Dawn continued on her intended path and as she approached Michelle opened her eyes and a beautiful smile broke across her lips.

"Hi." She murmured, seeming half in a trance still.

"Hey." Dawn folded her long legs and sat down, not taking her eyes off Michelle. She could hear the rest of the class moving around signaling the end of the breathing session.

"I hope everyone enjoyed themselves today. Remember I'll be here tomorrow at the same time if you would like to join me." Dell's soothing voice broke through the quiet conversations that had started around them. "If you start getting overwhelmed, just ground and center and feel your breaths. It will help. You don't have to rush away rush away because class is over, sit, take your time, enjoy the view and be one with Mother Nature."

Michelle had been focusing on Dell and now she

turned her expressive brown eyes towards Dawn. Since she didn't seem to be in a rush to leave Dawn stretched her legs out and idly toyed with a piece of grass.

"Did you enjoy meditation class?" Dawn asked.

"I did." Surprise tinged Michelle's voice. "Honestly when we started I felt kind of weird, really hokey. But in the end I relaxed." She paused and leaned in to whisper. "I'm glad I didn't fall asleep. That would have been rather embarrassing."

Dawn snickered and reached and took Michelle's hand in her own. "You look beautiful by the way." She whispered and then leaned back taking in the five other students as they gathered their belongings. Having met most of them previously Dawn smiled a greeting and kept tight hold of Michelle's hand as they gathered up the yoga mats and began to move away.

Cathy separated from the group and strode over. "Michelle. I'm glad you came today."

"Me too." Michelle smiled up at the woman. "You remember my friend Dawn?" She dipped her head towards Dawn with a soft smile.

"I do. How come you didn't join us in meditation?" Cathy had an easy going soft face and clear blue eyes as she spoke to Dawn.

"Oh meditation isn't really my thing. Also Michelle

needed some time away from us." Dawn pegged Cathy to be approximately forty five. She wore jogging pant capris and a loose white tank top that spoke of a comfort with herself and a confidence that suggested she might be a professional. Dawn let her gaze skim over her and noticed the slightly whiter skin on her ring finger and a pang of compassion flowed through her. She assumed the woman to be either newly divorced or widowed.

"I'm glad Michelle came today." She grinned infectiously. "At least I wasn't the only newbie. Anyways you have a great day and maybe I'll see you at dinner."

As Cathy moved away Michelle turned towards Dawn a soft smile on her lips. "I am so relaxed I could melt, and both Dell and Cathy seem nice. I'll admit to being nervous," she grinned, "but I got over that."

"Nothing to be nervous about. Dell is great, which I told you, Whispering Winds is like a second home to her. And Calia only offers the best in classes and seminars, it is after all her reputation on the line. Do you want to head back now?" Dawn asked entwining her fingers with Michelle's as she spoke.

"Do you mind if we stay here for a bit? I don't want to move yet."

"Anything you want." Dawn watched the sunlight play on Michelle's skin for long moments allowing contentment and peace to fill her. After a few minutes Michelle started fidgeting slightly and Dawn could tell she needed to talk about something. She waited patiently, not wanting to push and instead let Michelle form her thoughts into words.

"I want to apologize for last night." Michelle's barely audible voice caught on the wind.

Dawn forced herself not to give in to her first reaction and jump up or yell. "What do you mean?" She asked instead.

"Neither you nor Mason got anything. You made it all about me." She muttered and hung her head as dark red smudges formed on her cheeks.

"Pease explain."

"I didn't even touch either of you, and Mason didn't get to... you know." Michelle hung her head, letting her hair create a shield between them. "There was no reciprocal pleasure. I feel horribly guilty."

Dawn took a moment to think about her response before speaking. "You were in our minds were you not?" Michelle nodded. "So then you know for a fact that I orgasmed, as did Mason."

"But I didn't do anything!" Michelle wailed.

"Just being with you is enough for us. I know I speak for Mason as well. It's not like we will be keeping a score card. Sometimes I will pleasure you and others you will pleasure me, sometimes we might do it both at the same time. Last night we wanted you to have a good sexual experience, probably your first one. That gave us joy, gave us pleasure. Seeing your face as ecstasy rushed through your body and took over will always be more than enough for me."

"But-"

"No buts." Dawn put a finger to her lips and brushed her hair back behind her ear. "We told you before there are no rules when it comes to us. We want you as you are, not trying to keep things even. You will have plenty of time. Trust me I cannot wait to have your hands all over me, last night we wanted to focus on making you comfortable with us. There was not, and there will never be any pressure."

Michelle thought that over for a few minutes and finally nodded. "Okay. I have a question though."

"Anything, baby." Dawn smiled.

"So, will it always be all three of us? Or will it sometimes be one on one? I don't get how to do this."

Dawn laughed lightly. "This isn't a game, this is life, and there are no rules. One action doesn't require a payback or obligation. We do things that pleasure us, in the moment, not thinking 'if I do this now, she'll do that later.' Sometimes it will be you and me, sometimes you and Mason. And sometimes it will be all three of us. We aren't keeping score." She reiterated.

"But won't it be weird? Won't there be jealousy?"

"How can I possibly be jealous of the other half of my soul? How could I possibly feel bad when you take pleasure with one another? Mason has parts I don't, and I," She grinned evilly and waggled an eyebrow. "I have skills he can't possibly dream of having. Our goal is for you to be happy. You are our soul mate and we are here for you, however you might need us. No jealousy. No judgement. Just pure and simple pleasure to have you with us."

"Oh." Michelle blushed prettily once more looking away.

"Don't worry so much." Dawn ran a finger down Michelle's cheek cupping her chin gently and turning her face so they were looking eye to eye. "There is no right or wrong. There is only us and we will find a way to make this work."

Michelle smiled and leaned in closer taking Dawn by surprise as she kissed her. Groaning happily Dawn let Michelle control the kiss. The tentative nips and licks from Michelle's gentle mouth combined with the warmth of the sun on her back and heated her system thoroughly. Michelle cupped Dawns face between her hands and opened her mouth allowing her tongue to possess every inch of Dawn's mouth.

With a sigh of pleasure Dawn gave in to the kiss letting her emotions, her love for Michelle come through.

~~~

$\mathcal{M}$ichelle thought about everything she had talked over with Dawn earlier and smiled happily as she lathered up her body. The hot water in the shower relaxed her body and steam filled the air.

Last night had awakened sensations inside her that she hadn't known were possible; lust, desire and a deep connection between the three of them that prior to meeting the Cubus she hadn't thought she would experience. It truly seemed as though Dawn and Mason were willing to take her as she was. That they loved her, damage and all.

As her mind and body healed from the horrors of her incarceration she found herself shocked to discover the person that hid beneath. Michelle had never thought much beyond her bare survival and now she had found that she could be a real person. A person worthy of both love and respect. A person who had thoughts and dreams, who deserved to be heard. Her realistic fear of what the future held always tinged at the back of her brain, however a spirit inside her, unknown before now refused to give up. She'd only ever seen herself as a victim and now when she looked in the mirror she saw a survivor.

For so long she had hidden away, terrified of Phelon and the people in the carnival. She had hidden from her emotions, knowing they could only hurt her. She never thought love, sex and emotions would be something she could experience. One night with Mason and Dawn and she knew she could never go back into the box that had been her life before them. She could never return to the scared little girl she had been. She wanted to experience life, to have the light of the moon dance on her face, to go back to school, to become the adult woman she had dreamt of being for so long.

She would love, and be loved, she would accept all the heart aches and joys of being a real person. She refused to be the paper doll any longer. She wouldn't accept being hidden away and only taken out when needed, she wouldn't take being used any more. Even if something untoward were to happen she refused to ever go back to the half-life she had led for so long. She would rather die.

Michelle knew she had been given a second chance at this life and she refused to let it slip past her. Today she took control, she would take a chance and she wanted nothing more than to be with her mates. Michelle blushed at the thought but knew for her sake she had to be the instigator. She needed to choose to be with them. To be an active part in the lovemaking, even if embarrassment nearly overcame her at the thought. She had spent most of the breathing class thinking about it and while Dawn had eased many of her concerns, she knew she had to do this.

The one thing that she figured would make it easier would be if she took the initiative one on one. When the two of them were there, they overwhelmed her, until she could only live in the moment. Their pure attractiveness, their charisma and mind boggling beauty, while wonderful and reassuring it became too overpowering, she couldn't think or act when they were together. She also suspected Mason was holding back. He had the sense of caution that seeped through their bond, a feeling of unease or fear that Michelle was determined to get to the bottom of.

Michelle quickly finished rinsing her body and stepped out of the shower, decision made. She took a deep breath and stepped out into the bathroom shivering slightly as the cooler air hit her skin. The fluffy towel luxuriously rubbed against her skin, skin that she smiled to see returning to its former golden state, the evidence of her beating disappearing with each passing day. Only faint smudges appeared where the darkest of bruises had been.

Finally after drying and combing her hair, brushing her teeth and fortifying her courage with the small acts of dressing she stepped out into the living room. As before her shower Mason sat in a chair watching the television distractedly. Dawn had left to check in with Calia.

She cleared her throat as she sat down and Mason looked up. "I wondered something."

"I will answer any questions you have, my Solotke." Mason's voice rumbled, deep and reassuring.

"Well, we haven't talked a lot about what it means to be a Cubus. An Incubus, specifically. I understand what you do and how you feed and so on but I am wondering if you have an alternate form. I mean on television and in books, werewolves change into a different form. Vampires grow teeth and so on. So do you have a secret face that the world doesn't typically see?" Michelle asked her words tumbling together as she spoke.

Mason searched her face before answering. "Yes. We do have an alternate form. We remain in complete control while in that form however it is rarely something that we show."

"Why?"

"It can be upsetting. Scary even, if a human sees us without being prepared. We don't need to go into that form for any day to day purpose so it isn't something we just hang out as. We typically only change if there is a need to do so." Mason leaned forward and turned off the television as he focused on Michelle.

"What would the reasons be?"

"Well, extreme emotions can trigger the change. Also we have some built in defenses that come with our alternate form that we don't have in this form." He motioned at his wonderfully built form and for a moment Michelle oogled his perfect frame and forgot her questioning.

"Can I see?" she asked, forcing her focus to return.

"No." Mason's flat voice echoed in the room.

"Why not?" Michelle tilted her head, curious at his frank denial.

"I will not ever do anything that will scare you."

"Wait." Michelle interrupted holding up a hand. "I have good reasons for wanting to see it now. First there is a chance that I might see it in the future and it makes sense for me to see now when it is a controlled circumstance rather than when it is sprung upon me unsuspecting. Second, you have seen every side of me, good and bad. I need to prove to you and to myself that I can take it. That you don't scare me no matter how you look." She paused while Mason took in her words. "You've assured me that you remain in complete control while in this alternate, I believe you. Show me that my faith in you isn't misplaced. If I am going to have a life with you and Dawn, I need to prove to myself that I am strong enough to accept you in all your forms. Not only the pretty one that I like to see so much."

"You like this side of me, do you?" Mason grinned.

"Don't change the subject. You aren't going to put me off. I want to see." Michelle crossed her arms over her chest and schooled her features into a stern, determined face. Inside her nervousness trembled, ready to burst forward but she believed wholeheartedly in Mason and knew her trust wasn't misplaced.

Mason sat for a long time, his eyes searching Michelle's face while she waited patiently, holding her breath. This had become more than a testament of her belief in him, it had also become a test of her strength. If she screamed or negatively reacted she knew it would damage not only her self-confidence but also Mason's ability to believe that she could handle herself. More than anything Michelle didn't want to be the fainting maiden who needed to be rescued at every turn. She wanted to be a strong woman who could ensure her own safety.

Finally Mason nodded. "You're right. You should see me when we can control the situation. That way if I ever change you won't be too scared. You need to know me in all my forms."

He stood facing Michelle and took a deep breath. "Are you ready?" Michelle nodded and clasped her hands together to prevent any sign of weakness or fear.

Mason threw his head back and the air around him seemed to shimmer. Michelle's eyes watered but she refused to blink, she wanted to see everything. Through the shimmer she could make out shifting on his face and around his hands. It only took a few seconds and then the glimmer faded, leaving only the faint light coming from the table lamps.

Mason lowered his head and his eyes met Michelle's. She took a breath and looked closely at his alternate form.

His eyes glowed a bright unnatural yellow, his skin had taken on a paler sheen. From behind his lips, a row of sharp pointed teeth protruded. She let her gaze go down to his hands where lethal looking claws extended from his fingertips.

She could tell he held his breath, nearly shaking with nerves about her reaction. She stood and circled around him, feigning an ease that she didn't feel. Mason stood without moving while she checked him over. Getting used to the Incubus side of him made her want to run away, and she fought the urge, refusing to be terrified or let her fear show. With exaggerated care she took her time adjusting to the new face, the new form. Her heart slowed to its normal pace, and her breathing calmed as she tilted her head looking at Mason from all angles. Behind the changes she still saw Mason. Finally she circled back to stand in front of him.

"What no tail?" She asked with an impish grin.

Mason's mouth dropped open in shock and he didn't speak.

"I guess I should have asked if you were able to speak in this form, huh?" Michelle's brow creased.

"I can talk." Mason said, his voice was lower and more guttural, feral almost, but she could still recognize the voice. "You shocked me."

"Okay. So you look different. However you are still

you." She reached up and touched his face gently. "I'm all right. Thank you for trusting me." She slid her hand into his multi colored hair and pulled his face towards her.

When his breath brushed across her skin she raised on her tip toes and placed a soft kiss on his lips. "You are the hottest man I've seen, this form or any other."

Mason groaned and closed his eyes. "Thank you." He whispered simply and then the air seemed to tighten around Michelle and she opened her eyes to see Mason in his human form. Her fingers laced through his hair and she pulled him closer until her body pressed against his intimately.

With a sigh she stepped away. "There is something else I need to talk about."

Wariness whipped across his features once again, which he quickly schooled into impassivity. "Okay. I am listening." He also stepped away putting enough distance between them that Michelle could think once more.

"What are you holding back?" She took the bull by the proverbial horns and asked.

"I'm not holding back." Mason shook his head in denial.

"Bullshit." Michelle crossed her arms over her chest defiantly. "I can feel what you feel Mason. I know you are hiding something. Something you are terrified will scare me off, or disgust me. Or I don't know, something you think I can't handle maybe. I just know something isn't right in that head of yours. You need to be totally honest with me. What is it you are hiding?"

Shame filled his eyes and he dropped her gaze. "Dammit. I didn't know you would be able to tell."

"I can't entirely. But I know something is up. Please trust me enough to tell me about whatever it is." Michelle pleaded.

After long moments Mason finally looked up at her and nodded. "You have a right to know." His posture spelled defeat as he moved to the couch and sat motioning for Michelle to join him. "The one thing you never asked was why Dawn and I were here at Whispering Winds when you arrived."

"I assumed you were visiting Calia, being that you are old friends." Michelle answered taking Mason's hand in her own, showing her support.

He shook his head again as he spoke. "Calia is an old friend but we weren't here just visiting. We were running away." He paused so long the silence took on a life of its own until finally he spoke again. "I don't know if you remember Dawn saying that I used to be a bartender but I was. Until very recently. I worked at a bar in Toronto. I've been there for years, I loved it. It used to be a pub full of great energy that I could feed on when needed but it never overwhelmed me. Then last year it got sold. The new

91

owners took my lovely little pub and turned it into a nightclub. The thumping techno music and gyrating bodies all that belong in a dance bar. Along with all that came these emotions. They were too much." Mason's voice tripped over itself as he seemed unable to breathe as he spoke. "There was so much. Lust, anger, jealousy, fear, distress. They swamped me and I lost control." He swallowed audibly. "I didn't mean to, but I couldn't stop. I started sucking up their emotions and I wouldn't have been satisfied until they were all dead, just to shut off the emotions that they were sending. Luckily Dawn came by and managed to knock me to my senses. But it was too late. She brought me here to get over it the next day."

"Oh no, Mason." Michelle felt nothing but love as she clutched his hand tightly.

"I put thirty two people in the hospital that night and drained an additional thirty eight to the point of exhaustion." Mason's voice was dead. "Without intending to I hurt seventy people. I would have killed them all."

"But you didn't." Michelle touched his chin forcing him to look at her. "You didn't."

"I could have."

"You didn't." Her voice firm she continued. "You lost control and who knows if you would have come to your senses on your own or not either way the point is moot. You were stopped. You didn't intend to hurt them, it just happened. It was an accident. I don't blame you."

"I almost didn't help you, I was afraid of what might happen." His low voice told Michelle just how deeply affected he was. "I refused at first and was very angry at Calia for bringing this problem to my door. All I wanted was to be left alone and to fade into the background."

"I am gladder than ever that she brought me to you." Michelle whispered. "You have done so much to help me and you should never fade away."

"Me as well. Because as much as we've healed you, you've healed me too." Michelle shook her head in denial but Mason continued. "You did. You gave me hope, you helped me gain control and comfort with my abilities once more. I felt myself pulling away from the world, getting ready to die but then you came in and changed everything. You accept me. What more could I need?"

Michelle smiled through the mist that had filled her eyes, for once she experienced a sense of total comfort with a man, and she had no fear either for herself or of him. She knew in places deep inside her that Mason would never hurt her, he would stand beside her, protecting her when she needed it, but more importantly backing her up when she could stand on her own. He was made for her.

She opened the mental connection between them and let all the emotions that overwhelmed her flow through it to Mason as she pulled him closer and kissed his lips passionately.

~~~

*M*ason couldn't believe his luck, terror had filled him at the thought of scaring Michelle, and yet she had shown him how strong she could be. His nerves nearly had him refusing to show her his Incubus alternate self, now he found himself floored by her reaction. Let alone his confession to almost killing a whole slew of humans. She accepted him, in all his shapes. Not only did she accept him but she had touched and even kissed him when he hadn't looked remotely human. She looked beneath the fangs and weird skin tone and saw him.

Now she kissed him, filling the link between them with nothing short of love. She may not have used the words yet, but words were unnecessary when he could feel the emotion running through her.

He groaned and returned the kiss letting his lust overwhelm him, forgetting to restrain himself, forgetting to worry about her. The undeniable passion that spurred between them took over. Their mouths fused together in a dance as old as time. He let Michelle lead and he followed, his tongue dueling with hers as they came to know one another.

Finally panting with lust he pulled away, resting his forehead against hers. "If we don't stop now, I won't want to ever stop." His voice sounded husky to his ears.

"Maybe I don't want to stop." Michelle whispered raising her determination and lust filled eyes to meet his.

"Solotke." He groaned.

"Come with me." Michelle took his hand and led him to the bedroom, where soft light diffused the room, the shadows licking at her profile as she turned to him.

"Are you sure?" He asked, even though his entire being screamed at him not to give up the opportunity she had presented him.

She nodded and he breathed a sigh of relief, which quickly sucked back into his lungs as she slid her hands beneath his shirt and caressed his stomach muscles. "Let me take control." She whispered.

He couldn't speak so he tilted his head in the affirmative instead and forced his hands into loose fists while he waited for her move. She ran her fingers lightly over his stomach causing him to contract his ab muscles involuntarily. His dick throbbed painfully behind the zipper of his jeans and for a moment he worried he might explode, with an iron will he clamped down on his libido and stood still.

She traced the defined muscles of his stomach slowly working her way to his chest, by the time she reached the flat disks of his nipples his breath ripped from his mouth in an uneven staccato. She traced and teased until Mason thought he would lose his mind.

She looked up at him with a frown on her pretty lips. "You're too tall, I can't take your shirt off."

"Oh Solotke all you have to do is ask." Nearly ripping his t-shirt in his haste Mason pulled the offending material off and tossed it on the floor before lowering his hands to his side once more. "And they do say we are all the same height when laying down."

"Well then." She took a step back and Mason nearly moaned in distress at the distance. "Perhaps our best plan would be to lay down." Mason started to move towards the bed when her voice stopped him in his tracks. "Naked."

He fought to control his breath as he looked in her eyes and saw nothing but a reflected desire. Once he had assured himself that she still wanted him with her mind as well as her body, he popped the button on his jeans and pushed them and his boxer briefs down his legs leaving them on the floor. Michelle's breath hitched as she looked over his body frankly and with approval.

He sat on the edge of the bed and watched as Michelle quickly divested herself of her clothes, also leaving a pile on the floor before she stepped up to him. Her softly curved body glowed red in the light, leaving a hole in his chest where his heart had once been, he knew he'd never seen anything as beautiful as Michelle. She placed her tiny hands on his chest and leaned in for a kiss.

Their lips met in a flurry of activity, and Mason couldn't resist placing his hands on her rounded bottom. The skin beneath his fingers, like sun warmed silk and he moaned into her mouth, his lust spiking his movements. Her hands pushed on his chest and he tumbled backwards on the bed, taking her with him, their lips still locked together. Her breasts pushed against him, inflaming him until he thought he would explode.

As though she sensed how close to detonation he had become Michelle pulled away and licked her way down his chest taking her time to lave attention one at a time on his nipples. Her fingers and lips were everywhere, touching, skimming, and caressing building him higher once again. Unable to resist he allowed his hands to touch her wherever she came within reach, smoothing the skin of her shoulders and back and peaking around to slide over her breasts.

Finally she pulled away and looked at him. "You are wonderful, Mason." Her voice murmured as it ran over his skin. "But you need to stop touching me, this is my show." An adorable crooked smile touched her lips.

"Alright." He exhaled. "I'll try. You're just so irresistible." Grinning ruefully, he forcibly removed his hands and placed them along his hips.

"Well how about this then," she amended "you can only touch me when I direct you to do so." She grinned and threw a leg over his stomach straddling him. Her warmed core touched his stomach muscles and he nearly cried out at the sensation. Moisture dripped from her and he had to fight to not lift her and slide her down the full length of his cock.

His eyes were closed as the sensations rippled over him. "Ahem." He flashed his eyes open and looked up realizing she waited on a response. He wracked his brains until he remembered they had been talking about her telling him what to do.

He cleared his throat. "Anything you say, O Captain my Captain."

A grin dimpled her cheeks. "You did not just quote Dead Poets Society at me. It's one of my favorite movies."

"You are totally in charge. Whatever you say goes." He grinned back. "So tell me Captain where would you like me to touch you?"

She appeared to think for a minute and sat back her back brushing against the tip of his painfully engorged member. He breathed through it, instead focusing on the beauty in front of him.

"How about if you start here." She raised her hands and cupped her full breasts, holding them like a present for him, the puckered dusky tips peeking through her fingers.

"Anything you say, O Captain my Captain." He murmured and raised his hands, letting his fingers brush the underside. He saw the goose bumps raise on her arms as she dropped her hands. He brushed along the outer edge of her perfect globes and heard her sigh. Slowly he worked his way to her nipples, gently caressing until they stood at perfect attention. Unable to resist he pulled lightly on the perfect peaks, rolling them between his fingertips until she moaned. Her hands mimicked his motions on his own chest and he pulled a little harder eliciting a gasp of pleasure from both of them. His eyes never left her face, the reddened skin flushed more with desire, the parted full lips being bitten between her teeth as she lost herself in the passion.

"What next?" He asked with a choked voice.

She looked at him with desire heavy in her eyes as she responded with a husky voice. "Perhaps we should move a little further south." She leaned back causing his cock to rest between the cheeks of her perfect ass, and spread her nether lips to his view. He could see her clitoris, swollen and glistening with her desire and he groaned unable to hold back.

"If that is what my lady requires of me, then god forbid I should deny her anything her heart desires." He knew instinctively that he wanted to keep it light for as long as possible so that she wouldn't revert to her past experiences. More than anything Mason wanted this to be the two of them in this bed and that her tormentors would remain in the past, forgotten as they deserved to be, with no power over her.

He let his hands drift along her ribcage, slowly teasing

her belly button before letting the soft crinkling hair covering her mound tickle his fingertips. With a sigh he circled her bud letting her wetness coat his fingers with slippery goodness. He used one hand to hold open her lips with the other worked her clit until she moaned and ground against him.

Her hand crept behind her and circled his length. "You shouldn't be the only one having all the fun." She muttered as she slowly worked her hand up and down gently, the slick pre-cum easing her movements. Mason squeezed his eyes shut, filled with a desire so strong it took everything he had not to buck into her hand. Although he wanted to go hard and fast, he followed Michelle's lead and let her set the pace.

Silence descended over them, the only sound in the room their harsh breathing as they touched one another with increasing urgency. For what seemed like forever they touched each other, losing themselves in pure sensation.

Michelle gasped, the sound music to Mason's ears as he tried to focus on her and her pleasure rather than what her magical hand were doing to him. She leaned further back and Mason took her meaning, teasing her entrance with a finger, nearly cooing at the wetness. He slowly eased in a finger, thrusting lightly into her tight channel. She moaned and threw her head back at the sensations.

"What next?" He forced himself to ask lightly.

Michelle's eyes flew open and she gazed at him, as though drugged.

"I need you inside me." She whispered.

"I want nothing more." He agreed. She shifted, confusion in her eyes as she tried to move so that she could ride him.

"Allow me to help?" He asked, to which she nodded. He grasped her hips and lifted her frame until his cock stood at attention, poised at her entrance. She reached down and positioned him perfectly. Her wetness coated the head of his penis, and torment filled him, he wished the moment could last forever and yet wanted to be inside her warmth immediately. He fought against his warring needs and waited holding his breath for a sign from Michelle. Finally she looked down at him and with a nod she slowly lowered herself onto him. Inch by inch, the muscles of her pussy tightened around him encasing him in her heat. She kept eye contact with him the entire time, her hands on his chest. Mason knew he wasn't a small man and he worried briefly that he would hurt her as she raised and lowered herself a few more times until finally she seated him fully inside her with a groan of pleasure.

"Perfection." He muttered, reminding himself to be gentle he loosened his grasp on her hips. She began to move and all thought battered from his mind. She set a frantic and harsh pace, as they both dove towards their pleasure.

Michelle grabbed his hands and placed them once more on her breasts as they bounced delightfully in front of him. She continued her wild thrusting, throwing herself down his shaft as though unable to control herself. His balls drew up, and a tingling shot straight up his spine signaling his orgasm was terribly close, he snaked his hand between her legs and pressed firmly against her hot spot. She let out a scream and her internal muscles spasmed as her orgasm took hold of her. He thrust up into her three more times and let loose with his release bathing her inner channel with his seed.

She collapsed on top of him gasping to catch her breath and Mason felt the pulse of her fluttering heartbeat as he fought to catch his own breath. He sighed with contentment and caressed her back lightly as they came down from the incredible high of being together.

After a few minutes she raised her head and rested it on the palm of her hand a speculative look on her face.

"What?" He asked lightly.

"Is it always like that?" She asked.

"Not always, Solotke, but when you are with someone you are meant to be with, magic happens. For us it will always be like that." He let his fingers lazily drift over her cooling skin.

"You know the idea of forever with you is growing on me." She sighed and dropped her head to his chest. Her breathing slowed and Mason watched as sleep overtook her, knowing his woman, perfect and sated, slumbered in his arms.

~~~

*M*ichelle grinned happily up at Dawn as they walked up to the pavilion, the crunch of pine needles beneath their feet. Mason had gone to talk with Ray and Calia, and would be joining them and Cathy for lunch. The past days had been an education for Michelle, she had learned that she had a sensual side and loved being touched. Being surrounded by the care that Dawn and Mason had shown her twenty four seven had let her stretch her wings and discover things about herself that she had never had the chance to know before. She hadn't used the 'L' word yet, but she knew without doubt that she loved the two of them and that they were meant to be together.

When Dawn had walked in to discover Michelle asleep on top of a naked Mason at first she had worried, even though she had been assured otherwise, that Dawn would be upset. To the contrary she had smiled and joined in for another round of loving that still left Michelle giddy. Between Dawn and Mason she had discovered how sensual she could be, they had christened nearly every surface in the cottage. She couldn't keep her hands to herself and her fears from the past had nearly dissipated entirely.

Michelle awoke each morning and had to take a moment to make sure she had escaped the trailer. She made sure it hadn't all been a dream, and she had indeed escaped. Sometimes it took longer than others, but eventually she realized the truth. Freedom. A strong gentle man and a beautiful woman who cared about her and were helping her become real. Each moment she spent with them reiterated the fact that she could live a life like any other person.

They entered the open air dining area, the light breeze breathing through the space. Dawn carried a picnic basket filled with all the fixings for sandwiches and a small bottle of wine.

They had eaten lunch with Cathy yesterday, and she had provided their meal so today they were reciprocating her generosity. She already awaited them, waving from what they now considered their table. She wore comfortable dark grey slacks and a light blue blouse that matched her eyes perfectly.

"Cathy, you look very nice today." Michelle pulled up a seat across from Cathy with a smile.

"Thank you." Cathy turned to Dawn. "Hello Dawn, nice to see you again. I am very glad you made it, I was getting worried I'd be on my own for lunch. My muse is being stubborn, so any distraction is valuable."

"Well, we're here now and thrilled to be your distraction." Dawn sat beside Michelle and took her hand with the ease of a long time relationship. Michelle's heart fluttered, she was still googly around Dawn, she couldn't help it. While she wore simple enough jeans and a comfortable t-shirt, she had the body that most women would die for. Her eyes were captivating, wide and fringed with thick black lashes that made Michelle swoon, add in the severe pixie haircut and her eyes stood out. She couldn't believe that this gorgeous specimen of a woman wanted her, she had started to comprehend the intensity, the deep emotions, but she found it difficult, every so often she couldn't help but be taken aback by the woman standing next to her.

"And just where is that big old hunk of yours?" Cathy looked around.

"Mason will be joining us in a few minutes. He had some work to attend to." Dawn scanned the area for a few seconds before relaxing her stance and turning back to her dinner companions.

"Are you coming to meditation class tomorrow?" Cathy asked.

"I think so." Michelle paused. "I did end up enjoying it more than I thought I would."

"Would you like to meet before class? We could walk together?" Cathy took a drink from the wine glass that Dawn handed her.

105

"Um." Michelle knew Dawn and Mason wouldn't let her out of their sight and didn't know how to phrase her answer.

"Unfortunately Michelle has other obligations that will keep her occupied right up until class starts. She'll be there; but it would be better to meet you at the pasture." As Dawn spoke she squeezed Michelle's hand reassuringly.

"Oh, okay, no big deal. I hate arriving alone to these things. As long as you are coming that's all I need to know." Cathy's wide clear blue eyes connected with Michelle's comfortably.

"Well, I will be there. Barring any problems in my other uh, obligations." Michelle looked up and saw Mason walking towards them. As always he drew the attention of any woman in the surrounding area, his commanding presence and model like good looks made it impossible not to watch him. Behind him stood a man Michelle hadn't seen before. She shrank slightly before realizing Mason would never bring anyone who would hurt her so she straightened up and took a fortifying breath.

"Michelle, Dawn, Cathy." Mason nodded to each woman in turn before returning his attention to Michelle. "This is Timothy Brumbacher. Ray asked us to chat with him."

Michelle looked closer at Timothy while the others greeted him and seats were shuffled to include the unexpected dinner companion. He looked to be in his late twenties, with thick pitch black hair kept trimmed above his ears in a professional style. His eyes were brown and slightly too close together giving him a hard look. Michelle pegged him at a hair under six foot, with a long and lean build. He had muscles but not bulk, overall he had the appearance of a good, if harsh looking man. Frankly he scared the hell out of Michelle and she knew the fear came from him being male, not because of anything wrong with him. He didn't look evil, he didn't look like he wanted to hurt Michelle but she couldn't help the fissure of fear that filled her when she looked at him.

Forcing herself to be brave, she ate her lunch while listening to the others talk. She participated in the pleasant conversation as minimally as possible. Nerves filled her about what part of her therapy this Timothy would be helping with even though both Dawn and Mason were sending her reassuring vibes through their bond. She still found herself imagining the worst.

Finally Cathy smiled and stretched. "That was absolutely delicious. Thank you for providing the meal. I'm so full I could bust a button." She patted her stomach with a laugh. "I am so glad I met you Michelle, and that you've introduced me to these lovely folks." She waved a hand around the table. "I'm definitely not as lonely as when I first arrived." She pushed back her chair and stood. "But it is time for me to retire. Thank you for all your company and conversation. Nice to meet you, Timothy."

Everyone said their good byes and Michelle smiled

faintly. "I'll see you at class tomorrow. Have a good day Cathy."

"See ya." Cathy waved as she moved out of the pavilion.

Mason took a quick look around and once satisfied no one could over hear the conversation he spoke. "Michelle, Timothy is from the HPC."

"The hidden police?" Michelle asked.

"Essentially yes." Mason grasped the hand that Dawn wasn't holding. "He is here to check on the hooks that Phelon put in. Ray called him in as a favor, he is a warlock, and we are hoping he can break the bond Phelon forced."

"So you're Tim the enchanter?" Michelle made the feeble joke hoping it would dissipate some of the seriousness in the room.

Everyone looked at her oddly, apparently not fans of Monty Python. "I prefer Timothy, and I am a warlock, not an enchanter." Timothy tilted his head as he looked at Michelle. "I've come at the behest of the HPC as well as Ray. They've asked me to try to help, I have been apprised of your situation. I cannot promise it will work, but I am going to give it my best. I am the strongest warlock the HPC has working for them at present, and I don't hesitate to say that I am the best. If I can't simply remove the hooks, I will figure out another way." His eyes were earnest and

Michelle nodded.

"Okay, when are we doing this? And where?" Michelle hated how weak her voice sounded but couldn't help herself.

"I think we'll attempt it today. Or at least let me see what is there. It would be best in private, Mason tells me you are staying in a house here at the retreat?" Michelle nodded. "That would be the best place then, very little chance of being interrupted."

They all agreed and left the building. Mason led the way to the golf cart and they piled in for the ride back to the cottage. As they drove Michelle watched the scenery. The sun had just set and the still faint pink light filled the sky, she could hear the river bubbling away in the distance. As they rounded the corner down the path to their accommodations she fought against the disappointment of missing another chance at going to the waterfall. She had heard so much about them thought they sounded truly amazing. A light had been left on in the fairy tale like cottage that they were living it, lending it a homey feel and directing them through the trees. Michelle breathed a sigh of relief, the deep sense of security that the cottage offered surprised her.

Once inside the living room seemed crowded with the four of them, but Michelle sat on the couch bravely. "So what do you need me to do?" She turned to Timothy, who sat opposite her in the same chair that last week she had sat, clutching a knife and meeting Mason and Dawn for the first time. Pride swelled up inside her, she had come so far in such a short time.

"May I?" He asked and motioned pulling the chair closer. Michelle nodded. Once he had situated the chair to his liking; so close their knees were almost touching he faced her. "You need do nothing. Just relax, that will make it easier. You don't feel the hooks, and you shouldn't experience any discomfort at the removal of them. There should be no pain, no discomfort and be relatively quick. The only thing I need to do is touch you."

Mason sat on one side of her, Dawn on the other and she could sense their concern. Their presence comforted her as she nodded to Timothy. "Let's do it then."

Timothy leaned forward and placed his fingertips on Michelle's temples. She jumped reflexively and both Mason and Dawn tightened their grips reassuringly. "Relax." Timothy murmured, his voice distracted.

"Sorry." Michelle forced herself to not move. She tried some of the breathing techniques Dell had taught her as Timothy closed his eyes and dropped his head, focusing internally.

For long moments they sat locked in silence as Timothy worked. A bead of sweat formed on his forehead and slowly dripped down the side of his face. True to his word, the session didn't hurt. His slightly sweaty fingertips pressed into her face firmly but without any pain, mental or physical and his slightly garlicy breath wafted over Michelle, distracting her from any lingering nerves. Breathing through her mouth Michelle focused on the wall behind him.

Finally he backed away, weariness pulling on his shoulders. Wiping a hand across his damp brow he pushed his chair back and turned to the trio sitting on the couch. With shock Michelle realized much more time had passed than she thought. The sky had darkened into the full pitch black of night.

He frowned and shook his head. "The hooks are still there. Whoever this Phelon is, he is an amazing warlock. I tried every trick I know and I could not get them to break free." He flopped back on the chair, exhaustion evident on his face.

Michelle suppressed a whimper and instead sat up straight. "So what do we do now?"

"On the way here I thought of every possible outcome and came up with contingency plans. I had hoped this would work, I have never failed before." He dropped his eyes. "For that I must apologize. But we must move on. The only other way to break the bond, or unhook his tethers if you will, is to meet with him."

Immediately Dawn and Mason shouted, "No!" and sprang to their feet. Michelle placed a hand on their backs, turning them to look at her.

"Let's hear him out." Her quiet voice sounded strong despite the lack of volume.

"Thank you, Michelle. If you meet with him, your bond with the Succubus here should automatically force the hooks out. The human mind can only maintain one life bond at a time, his is barely holding on and it is only holding on because it existed for so long and had been reinforced so many times. Once his magic's recognize the new bond they will retreat. Unfortunately the only way for his magic's to see the new bond is for him to see you, in the flesh."

The helpless teenager inside Michelle quaked at the thought and she really wanted to throw up. But the adult part of her knew she needed this to move on. She had the utmost faith in Dawn and Mason and their ability to keep her safe.

Slowly she nodded. "That makes sense."

"From reading the file on him and what you unwillingly did for him, I can't imagine he is too far away. The only thing keeping him from coming to the retreat is the magic's that protect it. I would imagine if you go into town he'll be waiting or at least real close by hoping to get you." Timothy looked at Mason and Dawn. "Don't worry, we will make sure she is protected. We will have trackers on her, both magical and mundane."

"If you think for one second we are letting her go alone, you'd be sorely mistaken." Dawn crossed her arms over her chest, defiantly.

"I think it's for the best that you two stay back." Timothy started and stopped when Mason interrupted him.

"No go. Either we are part of the plan or there is no plan. And trust me I know you want to catch him badly. The HPC wants him to pay for breaking the laws and misusing humans the way he did. If they don't catch him it looks bad on their authority. So no. There is absolutely nothing you can say that will convince us to let her go without us." His firm voice broke no arguments.

Timothy looked back and forth between them, finally capitulating. He nodded. "Fine. I'm going to head home, in order to come up with a plan. We have limited time, I want the action to be on our terms and if we wait too long he will find a way to turn the tables to his benefit." He stood and shook everyone's hand. "I'll talk to you tomorrow and we'll firm up what needs to be done."

~~~

Terror filled Dawn. She couldn't explain her emotional state any other way. She knew intellectually that the plan was necessary but that didn't prevent the fear. So many things could go wrong and she would lose Michelle. She glanced at the woman who walked beside her, trying not to hover, but she didn't even want to let go of her hand.

"Relax Dawn." Michelle's voice reached her. "I'm scared too, but we all know there is no other way. Let's enjoy the rest of our time here and try not to think about what comes next."

"Uh huh." Dawn muttered. "I'm trying."

Michelle stopped and faced her, wrapping her arms around Dawn's waist. She hugged her so tight it could almost be counted as uncomfortable and her words were muffled against Dawn's shoulder. "It will be okay. I refuse to believe that things will go wrong. I deserve a bit of good luck for a change, and now that I know what there is for me in this big bad world, I am not giving it up."

Dawn leaned in and inhaled the scent of her hair, faint melons with a mint undertone that both refreshed and uplifted. "You're right, of course. I'm sorry."

"Now I've been looking forward to seeing this fabulous waterfall since you guys first mentioned it, can we get going?" She grinned up at her and stretched on her toes to give her a light peck on the lips. "At this rate, Mason will beat us there, even after he runs Timothy back to the road and updates Calia."

Michelle turned and still holding Dawn's hand, led her through the forest. The well-marked path had small lights to make night visits easier. They rounded a corner and the path opened up to a breath taking sight. A large natural formation of rocks surrounded the bubbling pool with sheer sides that offered privacy. In the distance she could hear the waterfall tumbling down somewhere near the back of the pool. The humidity in the air told the tale of the warm water, it stuck to Michelle's throat comfortingly. There were strategically placed blue spotlights reflecting off the water giving a rainbow effect in the space.

Dawn grinned at Michelle and spotting strategically placed towel racks she watched as Michelle stripped down to the speedo style bathing suit Calia had so generously provided. With a deft hand she pulled her long hair into a loose bun on the top of her head. Dawn's mouth went dry, the modest speedo only seemed to enhance Michelle's full breasts giving them a curve that made Dawn's heart pound. Her skin glowed in the light, shown off to perfection by the black suit.

Dawn stood staring at the grounded, earthy beauty. Her mate. She walked over to the easily visible entry into the pool and put a foot in sighing with pleasure. Michelle slowly lowered herself into the pool and treaded over to a built in seat that ringed the edge. Dawn shook herself and quickly divested herself of her clothes. She knew her bright red halter style bikini showed off her legs and after a surreptitious glance making sure Michelle watched, she took her time getting into the pool. She had never been a jump into the pool kind of girl, she liked going slow, letting her fingers drift over the surface of the water, taking her time to become adjusted. She hid a grin as she saw the reflection from Michelle's dark eyes as they watched her intently.

She made her way towards Michelle noticing the water warming, she knew they must be near the underground source of the hot tub. The spring pulsed against her thighs a relaxing heat. Dawn sank down to the bench beside Michelle, her fingers automatically entwining with Michelle's below the surface. They sat soaking up the heat for long moments before Dawn smiled at the sound of running water and looking around she saw a curved back area that she hadn't seen before. She nudged Michelle, motioning towards the narrower area. "Wanna go check that out?"

Michelle nodded and Dawn swam down the stream like structure knowing Michelle followed. The comfortable water reached Dawns shoulders, about five feet, deep enough that swimming made movement easier. The warm water flowed against her skin as she moved through, although not as hot as it had been closer to the spring. The stream curved back into a horseshoe area that had a large water fall streaming cooler water into the pool. The rock walls climbed high in this area, leaving a sense of remoteness, almost like they were truly alone. The blue lights were still here but fainter lending an air of mystery to the grotto. She turned and realized how private the area had become when she could no longer see the main area of the pool.

Michelle swam closer and smiled at her shyly. "Did you bring me here to get me alone?" She asked.

Dawn shook her head, even as a shot of lust jolted

116

through her at the thought. "I brought you here because you asked. And because you needed to relax."

"You relax me." Michelle whispered as she circled her hands behind Dawn's neck. She kissed her passionately, her body pressed tight against Dawn's. Dawn moaned into her mouth and returned the kiss with fervor, her hands plunging into the loose bun of Michelle's silky hair.

Finally they pulled away looking at each other. "We can go back to the house." Dawn squeaked out.

Michelle shook her head, waving an arm at the high walls that surrounded them. "I think this is perfect."

"You sure?" Dawn asked.

Michelle nodded. "I reserved the pool for tonight when I spoke with Calia this morning. Apparently it is quite common for artists to want alone time in the hot tub. She assured me that we'd have no interruptions."

Dumbfounded Dawn could only stare at Michelle, astounded that she had been thinking about this all day and hadn't given it away.

"Did I surprise you?" Michelle grinned slyly.

"Uh huh, should we wait for Mason?" Dawn asked, praying that the answer would be no. Her breasts were tight with need and the throbbing between her legs had nothing to do with the heat of the pool and everything to do with the look in Michelle's eyes.

GLORIA C BISHOP

"No need." Mason's deep voice came from behind her and she almost jumped, only held still by Michelle's arms around her. "I'm here."

She turned with Michelle and they watched as Mason walked through the water with ease, his bare chest gleaming with water in the bluish lights. Michelle sighed beside her and Dawn smiled as the lust built in Michelle's mind.

Dawn backed her towards the shelf that served as seating and ran along the rock wall. As she went Dawn stripped the black swimsuit from Michelle's body and quickly tossed it to the side of the pool. Mason slipped up just as they reached the seat and swooped in for a deep kiss, his tongue tangling with Michelle's furiously.

Dawn unable to resist dropped her head and pulled one dusky tip into her mouth, while palming the other glorious breast in her other hand. From their joint bond the passion spiked boldly between them and she knew this wouldn't be some leisurely exploration of each other's bodies. All of them were nervous about the upcoming meeting and needed to possess each other, to declare the mating between them. They needed each other too bad to take their time.

Dawn suckled her breast firmly until turgid points formed and Michelle's breathing came out in harsh exhalations as she kissed Mason. Finally Michelle pulled away and motioned for Mason to strip, which he quickly

118

obeyed.

Dawn raised her hands to untie the necktie of her swim top but Michelle shook her head and pulled her closer. Michelle's tiny hands slid into the halter style swim top and teased Dawn's nipple until she threw her head back with the joy that overcame her. Damn that woman knew how to tease her, she quivered with the need to cum.

Her other hand made quick work of the hip ties holding her bottoms on and Dawn moaned as Michelle dragged the material through her legs, rubbing roughly against her clit. With a smile, Michelle tossed the swim bottoms to the side of the pool and deftly divested her of her top and it sailed over to join the pile of clothes.

The cooler air and slight overspray from the waterfall beside them coated Dawn's skin causing a round of goosebumps to cover her upper body. Her nipples pointed skywards and begged to be touched. Michelle did one better, she pulled Mason in to stand beside Dawn and leaning forward she took Dawn's nipple into her mouth and sucked intently. Dawn managed to remain standing as she saw Michelle's other hand stroking Mason under the water.

All three were breathing harshly under Michelle's riveting attentions. Finally Mason groaned and pulled away.

"Damn, Solotke." He muttered. "You need to stop or I'm going to blow before I even get to touch you."

Michelle grinned looking like the cat who ate all the

cream. "Wouldn't want that, now would we?" She looked up at Dawn. "I think you should hop up here." She patted the outcropping of rock that formed the back of the seating area.

Without hesitation Dawn jumped up, eagerness in her movements. She didn't care that the position left her almost entirely out of the water. Michelle turned her back on Mason and slowly skimmed her fingers along the skin of Dawn's calves. She circled her ankles and crawled onto the seat backwards. Her tiny pink tongue darted out and she licked a path up Dawn's legs. Dawn couldn't close her eyes, even if she wanted to; the sight before her, everything she'd ever wanted flickered in the faint light. So damned erotic she vowed not to miss a second of it. Michelle's back glistened with water, the globes of her ass skimming the water line as she knelt on the seat. Her hair messed and half falling down as she kissed Dawn's inner thigh.

"Oh Solotke. If only you knew how appealing you are right now." Mason crouched behind her, his face level with her ass as he teased his fingers down her spine. Dawn nodded emphatically in agreement.

Michelle didn't respond as her hands reached around firmly pulling Dawn by the hips to the edge of the ledge, forcing her legs wide around Michelle's body.

"Mmm." Michelle moaned. "So pretty." Her breath teased across Dawn's exposed flesh. "I love that you are shaved down here." She whispered just before her tongue delved between the folds of Dawn's labia and licked a path from her entrance straight to her clit. "And you taste so damned good." Michelle bent and suckled on her button of pleasure firmly.

At this point Dawn lost control and her eyes slammed shut as sensations stormed through her body. Michelle grasped her ass and anchored Dawn firmly against her lips, giving her tongue free reign on Dawn's pussy.

Bombarded by the sparks chasing along her skin, Dawn hooked a leg over Michelle's back giving her everything she wanted. "Yes." She hissed and opened her eyes to see Mason's fingers working Michelle's nether lips with a look of rapt attention to detail in his eyes.

Michelle moaned and thrust her tongue inside Dawn's channel. She pulled away and looked up at Dawn, her face glistening with the evidence of Dawn's pleasure. "Tell me you're close." Dawn nodded in agreement. "Good." Michelle turned her head and muttered. "Please Mason. I need you."

She turned back and plunged her face back between Dawn's legs, attacking her vag with passion evident in every swipe of her tongue. Dawn watched as Mason grasped Michelle's hips lifting them so that they were almost completely out of the water and level with his manhood.

With a groan from all three of them he pushed inside her. Michelle mumbled "Yes," against Dawn's clit and suckled the swollen bundle of nerves back into her mouth. Mason began thrusting from behind, his motions frantic and almost clumsy. Michelle worked one hand free and thrust a finger into Dawn's channel. She pumped a second finger in and began keeping time with Mason's motions.

Dawn grabbed Michelle's hair and held her against her shaven womanhood as an orgasm tingled behind her eyes. Together they thrust and moved against one another in a choreographed dance designed for them. Each chasing the orgasm that teetered just beyond their reach. Dawn threw her head to the side and the cooler water of the waterfall cascaded over her head dripping down her body to wet her further. She barely noticed the difference in temperature as every muscle in her body tightened begging for release.

Without effort the bond opened between them. Dawn knew how Michelle's tight channel gripped Mason's penis, pulling on him incessantly. She knew how Michelle loved the taste of her juices and how Mason thrusting deeply inside her, while his fingers tweaked Michelle's clit in time to the thrusts made her internal muscles quiver with desire. Michelle and Mason knew how utterly decadently Michelle's tongue slid against Dawn's clit. Together they felt one another and they were one. And as one they orgasmed in a loud cry of completion that melded together into one voice.

~~~

*M*ichelle grinned happily from the couch. She'd heard the waters at the falls were healing, but last night had beat all expectations, and she felt fully healed. Ready to take on Phelon and anything else the world threw at them. Tomorrow she would head into town. Timothy had called Mason and Calia to the office to go over a few more details while Dawn and Michelle remained at the cottage until breathing class. They were going to do another session of emotional healing if time permitted, Michelle figured it would help to feed the Cubus so they were strong enough to deal with anything; and a little more distance from memories of Phelon couldn't hurt.

Dawn had jumped in for a quick shower when a knock on the door caught Michelle's attention. She looked through the window and saw Cathy standing there ringing her hands.

Quickly she opened the door. "What's wrong?"

"Oh my God, thank god you're here. Mason's been hurt. Calia sent me to get you." Panic ringed the woman's eyes and she shifted from foot to foot anxiously.

"What happened?" Michelle's heart lunged against her chest.

"I don't know! Calia threw me the keys for a golf cart and sent me to get you. Hurry!" Cathy jumped off the porch and sped back towards the golf cart.

Torn, Michelle turned and yelled into the cottage. "Something's wrong with Mason. I've gone to find out what. Come as soon as you get out of the shower."

She ran down the stairs and threw herself into the golf cart with Cathy, who hit the gas pedal immediately, spinning the tires in her rush to turn the cart around.

Michelle twisted in her seat as they barreled down the path and caught a glimpse of Dawn running naked onto the porch. She turned back to Cathy. "Tell me what you know. Please." Terror filled her, she couldn't stand a life without either Mason or Dawn and she needed to be with him right now.

"I really don't know. I heard a loud noise and Calia and Mason ran out heading to the pasture. They were yelling something like 'how did he get into the retreat?' Next thing I know Calia runs back in and yells at me to get you and bring you them, before she took off again." She squealed around a corner so fast it Michelle thought they were on two wheels.

Michelle wracked her brain trying to figure out why they would have gone to the pasture. If her recollections were clear that was close to the parking lot and if Phelon had gotten in that would have been his access point to the property. She grabbed the holy shit handle and held on for dear life as they spun down narrow pathways barely avoiding being hit by tree branches.

She tried to open the bond between her and her mates and found it sticky, like it couldn't open properly. Although she couldn't send words she focused on her emotions. She forced through worry, anxiety and a vague sense of Mason. Immediately the same sense returned to her by Dawn but nothing from Mason which worried her even more. Then all connection with Dawn disappeared as well and Michelle whimpered at the loss of contact.

They screamed up to the far edge of the pasture and within sight of the parking lot and Michelle jumped out of the golf cart looking around frantically. Several cars were within sight but she couldn't see Mason or Calia anywhere. She turned back to Cathy.

"Where are they? Do you see them?" Her voice caught.

"They must be in the parking lot." Cathy followed as Michelle fought her way to run through the thick grasses that filled the space.

She slowed. "Wait. They wouldn't have gone into the parking lot. They told me never to step foot there without them. It isn't safe. What's going on?" She turned slowly back to Cathy who stopped with a sick grin on her face.

"Oh. It isn't safe." Her voice deepened and Michelle shivered, taking an involuntary step back.

"Who do you work for?" She whispered, afraid she already knew the answer.

Cathy laughed. "I don't work for anyone." She reached a hand up and with a loud ripping sound slowly peeled the skin down her face in a sickening mess of goo and blue spark of magic. She shuddered and the rest of the illusion fell away.

Michelle gasped as Phelon stood in front of her. His slight frame not much bigger than that of the woman he had chosen to impersonate, but his face, the face from her nightmares grinned back at her. The cold blue eyes, thin lips and blond hair in a ponytail down his back. The epitome of evil. He dropped the slimy skin that had been Cathy onto the ground without a second look.

"How?" She stuttered.

"Easily enough for a warlock like myself. Found poor little Cathy here, who had run into town to pick up supplies for her stay at the retreat, I took her skin and returned as her. The bitch owner doesn't check every time someone leaves. Only when they first arrive does she check for evil intent. Cathy here was the perfect mask." He kicked negligently at the skin he'd dropped.

"You killed her?" Michelle's voice rose.

"Of course. What was she, but merely human? I gave her pitiful life some purpose. I needed a way into the retreat after I figured out where you were."

"You are a monster." Michelle spat out.

"Not a monster, just better than human. Did you miss me? I told you, you were mine. You are going to regret running away. This time I will not go as easy on you as I have in the past. Now get in the damned car." Michelle shook her head and stumbled back as far away as she could manage.

"I said get in the car." His forehead scrunched up in a familiar way, he attempted to link to Michelle, like he had so many times before. Michelle flinched in fear, but felt nothing. Her heart leapt knowing the link had been destroyed. "You broke my bond. How did you manage that?" He scratched his chin as Michelle tried to move further away. "Of course, you bonded with someone else. The two leeches. You know I am shocked at what a little whore you turned out to be. I saw you last night you know. Taking on two at once, that's something. I think I might have to take you for a ride myself, after I beat the creature stench from you of course. Get in the car." His voice grew loud but Michelle only shook her head and backed up more.

"Fine. Be difficult."

He waved a hand and magic tethers sprung from his hands and wrapped around Michelle's upper arms in a band that tightened around her painfully as it lifted her up and began to carry her towards the parking lot. She screamed as loud as she could both physically and mentally as she struggled against the bonds holding her.

She drifted closer to the car and she screamed again, fighting with all her might. Her feet couldn't reach the ground and she couldn't escape the vise that held her. Panic filled her as she tried to formulate a plan. If he would come a little closer Michelle knew she could kick him, which might distract him enough to drop the magical straight jacket that held her captive.

"Let her go!" A voice called out and Michelle twisted her head to see Mason and Dawn in their full Cubus glory, claws and fangs extended, explode from the forest. Beside them bounded Calia, her fury evident as she sparkled green energy from her hands. The treetops swayed seemingly angry as well and trying in futility to reach Phelon. Michelle ignored Calia for the moment and focused instead on the sight of her mates.

"She belongs to me!" Phelon screamed, a bulging purple vein jumping out on his forehead.

"This is the end. Drop her." Mason's harsh voice menaced as the three moved towards them.

Phelon laughed maniacally and thrust his hand skyward. The air crackled and before anyone could move lightning struck the ground knocking Mason from his feet and throwing him ten feet across the sand. He landed with a loud thump and Michelle screamed when he didn't move.

Dawn and Calia split up circling around to the sides of Phelon as Michelle struggled against the bonds holding her, tears of fear and worry trailing down her cheeks. She couldn't tear her eyes from Mason's unmoving frame.

"Phelon." Dawn yelled drawing his gaze her way. "Let Michelle go. End this now and no one else has to get hurt."

"The only ones getting hurt will be you!" Phelon screamed, spittle foaming on his lips as he gestured again with his hand and the air around everyone tightened again. A loud crack shot through the air, the only warning they had as lightning struck again. Dawn jumped out of the way and the lightning narrowly missed her and struck the dead skin of Cathy where it lay on the grass. Once the smoke cleared Michelle could see that the lightning had completely eviscerated the poor woman's remains.

From the corner of her eye she saw Mason wobble to his feet and Michelle breathed a silent sigh of relief before training her eyes back on Phelon. Phelon panted and bent over slightly and Michelle's mind gave a shriek as he started to drain her energy. A faint sickly blue smoke began to leak from her body drifting across the sand to Phelon. As she weakened she could see Phelon straightening up, her stolen energy bolstering his personal reserves. She cried out unable to hold back the frustration at being held so helpless yet again while he used her energies. Her anger overwhelmed her, she hated that Phelon used her energies to hurt the people she loved.

"The HPC know about you. They will never stop hunting you. Give up now and they may be lenient on you." Dawn moved slightly closer, watching wearily for any sign of attack.

Phelon growled and jumped, grabbing at Michelle, she assumed to use her as a shield. However she had taken the time to get ready, and aimed a kick that knocked him away as Calia swung in from behind leaping an impossible distance and knocking Phelon to the side. Dawn also moved in and closing her fist she punched Phelon so hard his head cracked back and his eyes rolled back in his head. Immediately the bonds let her go and she slumped barely managing to stay on her feet. Mason ran up and encircled her in his arms.

"Mason." Michelle cried, "Are you alright?"

"I'm fine. A little singed but okay." Mason cringed and moved his body to partially block Phelon from view.

The Cubus shifted back to human form and the air crackled around Calia until the green sparks stopped sputtering from her fingertips. The tree tops stopped swaying towards them and the air became calm once again.

She paced between Phelon and them for long moments frustration evident in her jerky movements and the way she kept cracking her knuckles. "Killing one of my guests. Scum. I hadn't thought of that. Dammit. I have to be better. And poor Cathy." She motioned at the left overs of Cathy that smoldered on the grass. "What evil." She growled at the unmoving body of Phelon and began pacing again.

Dawn watched over Phelon ready to pounce again if he awoke, while Mason looked Michelle over, running his hands over her arms lightly. "Are you all right?" He asked. "Did he hurt you?"

Michelle shook her head. "I'm fine. Don't worry about me." Her voice shook and she pulled away from Mason making her way towards Phelon. Dawn hissed and Calia made to pull her away but she moved past them.

Faced with her greatest enemy she wanted to hit him, to hurt him as he had hurt her. She looked at his prone body and knew what she could do, but his unconscious body elicited no emotions, he no longer held her in his power, he wasn't worth her time. He had told her himself the bond had been broken and he couldn't hurt her anymore.

She turned away as Timothy rushed into the pasture and took over for Dawn. The HPC would make him pay. Instead she turned towards the three who had saved her.

"Thank you." She tilted her head to Calia, who calmer now merely smiled shaking her head as though gratitude was unnecessary and went to help Timothy.

"Come here." She whispered to Dawn and Mason who moved to her as quickly as they could. She put her arms around them and the three of them hugged each other fiercely. "I love you."

"Oh Solotke. You are my heart." Mason muttered in

131

one ear. "You scared us to death."

"You are everything to me." Dawn whispered in the other ear, squeezing her tightly.

Michelle smiled serenely knowing everything worked out exactly the way it was supposed to in the end. That everything she had been through had only led her to this moment, to this happiness. She would do more than survive, she would thrive and become a woman worthy of her Incubus and Succubus.

The End

ABOUT THE AUTHOR

Gloria lives in Southwestern Ontario Canada, with her hubby, her two teenage kids and a slightly larger than normal (or believable) cockapoo name Spike. She was lucky enough to meet the dude of her dreams at a drunken toga party while at college, two days before her nineteenth birthday and they've been together ever since. She believes in romance, and that attraction doesn't have to die off. She loves to laugh with her hubby and believes in keeping a sense of humor above all else. Gloria has always written, everything from poetry to a column in a local paper. Her favorite is to write romance, because everyone deserves that feeling, that belief in a happily ever after.

She draws and collects crafts like other women collect shoes (which she also collects but that's another story) When she isn't wearing her hat as mom, wife, writer, sister, artist, daughter, crafter, doggie mommy, friend – she can be found sitting around a campfire with an eclectic group of friends.

Over all she is a scooter riding, wookie hoodie wearing fun loving woman who refuses to grow up.

OTHER TITLES BY GLORIA C BISHOP

Supernaturally Yours

Anna is your average small town girl. She likes to cook works
at a bookstore, and is quiet, and klutzy -the girl next door.
She is also a supernatural creature.
Becoming a zombie has brought her nothing but heartache.
Her family life, her love life, even her self-esteem have been
shattered as a result of her transformation. After sitting on the
sidelines for far too long, Anna decides to begin dating again.
Unfortunately her foray into the world of supernatural
singledom is met with disaster.
Thrown into the arms of the one man who hurt her more than
any other by a psychopath bent on her destruction, Anna is
forced to reevaluate her opinion of Nathan. Their steamy
chemistry is overwhelming as they discover that together the
can find, and overcome, the fiend who is behind the attempts
on Anna's life.

Liquid Fire

Everyone remembers their childhood as being magical. Lee
just found out hers really was.
After suffering a run of bad luck, Lee wants nothing more than
to lick the wounds of her past and bury herself away from
reality, but she discovers a world of magic, a history she never
realized existed. Her destined elementals are being held against
their will and the only way to find them is to align with the
incredibly delectable, unbelievably stubborn Jeremy. They wind
down pathways that will take their undeniable chemistry even
higher as they move closer to the sinister plot that has stolen
her birthright. Together they will find the villain and learn that
sometimes fire and water can mix with steamy, hot results.
A spark of flame glows. A sprinkle of rains slows.

THE WHISPERING WINDS